Little Tongues of Fire

Vina was at the piano, softly playing.

"I am sure, Miss Wallace," the Duke said, "you express yourself more easily in music than in words."

Vina looked up at him as if she were surprised.

"I did not think anyone would understand . . ."

It suddenly came into the Duke's mind that Vina, with her strange beauty, had a perception which he knew was peculiarly prevalent in the East, where she was born.

As if he were waiting for an answer, Vina said:

"I try not to read people's secret thoughts . . . but I cannot help knowing what they are really like however hard they pretend to be . . . different."

She spoke quite ingenuously but to the Duke it was a warning . . .

A Camfield Novel of Love
by Barbara Cartland

Camfield Place,
Hatfield
Hertfordshire,
England

Dearest Reader,

Camfield Novels of Love mark a very exciting era of my books with Jove. They have already published nearly two hundred of my titles since they became my first publisher in America, and now all my original paperback romances in the future will be published exclusively by them.

As you already know, Camfield Place in Hertfordshire is my home, which originally existed in 1275, but was rebuilt in 1867 by the grandfather of Beatrix Potter.

It was here in this lovely house, with the best view in the county, that she wrote *The Tale of Peter Rabbit*. Mr. McGregor's garden is exactly as she described it. The door in the wall that the fat little rabbit could not squeeze underneath and the goldfish pool where the white cat sat twitching its tail are still there.

I had Camfield Place blessed when I came here in 1950 and was so happy with my husband until he died, and now with my children and grandchildren, that I know the atmosphere is filled with love and we have all been very lucky.

It is easy here to write of love and I know you will enjoy the Camfield Novels of Love. Their plots are definitely exciting and the covers very romantic. They come to you, like all my books, with love.

Bless you,

Barbara Cartland

CAMFIELD NOVELS OF LOVE

by Barbara Cartland

THE POOR GOVERNESS
WINGED VICTORY
LUCKY IN LOVE
LOVE AND THE MARQUIS
A MIRACLE IN MUSIC
LIGHT OF THE GODS
BRIDE TO A BRIGAND
LOVE COMES WEST
A WITCH'S SPELL
SECRETS
THE STORMS OF LOVE
MOONLIGHT ON THE
    SPHINX
WHITE LILAC
REVENGE OF THE HEART
THE ISLAND OF LOVE
THERESA AND A TIGER
LOVE IS HEAVEN
MIRACLE FOR A MADONNA
A VERY UNUSUAL WIFE
THE PERIL AND THE
    PRINCE
ALONE AND AFRAID

TEMPTATION OF A
    TEACHER
ROYAL PUNISHMENT
THE DEVILISH DECEPTION
PARADISE FOUND
LOVE IS A GAMBLE
A VICTORY FOR LOVE
LOOK WITH LOVE
NEVER FORGET LOVE
HELGA IN HIDING
SAFE AT LAST
HAUNTED
CROWNED WITH LOVE
ESCAPE
THE DEVIL DEFEATED
THE SECRET OF THE
    MOSQUE
A DREAM IN SPAIN
THE LOVE TRAP
LISTEN TO LOVE
THE GOLDEN CAGE
LOVE CASTS OUT FEAR
A WORLD OF LOVE

DANCING ON A RAINBOW
LOVE JOINS THE CLANS
AN ANGEL RUNS AWAY
FORCED TO MARRY
BEWILDERED IN BERLIN
WANTED—A WEDDING
    RING
THE EARL ESCAPES
STARLIGHT OVER TUNIS
THE LOVE PUZZLE
LOVE AND KISSES
SAPPHIRES IN SIAM
A CARETAKER OF LOVE
SECRETS OF THE HEART
RIDING IN THE SKY
LOVERS IN LISBON
LOVE IS INVINCIBLE
THE GODDESS OF LOVE
AN ADVENTURE OF LOVE
THE HERB FOR HAPPINESS
ONLY A DREAM
SAVED BY LOVE
LITTLE TONGUES OF FIRE

Other books by Barbara Cartland

THE ADVENTURER
AGAIN THIS RAPTURE
BARBARA CARTLAND'S
    BOOK OF BEAUTY AND
    HEALTH
BLUE HEATHER
BROKEN BARRIERS
THE CAPTIVE HEART
THE COIN OF LOVE
THE COMPLACENT WIFE
COUNT THE STARS
DESIRE OF THE HEART
DESPERATE DEFIANCE
THE DREAM WITHIN
ELIZABETHAN LOVER
THE ENCHANTED WALTZ
THE ENCHANTING EVIL
ESCAPE FROM PASSION
FOR ALL ETERNITY
A GOLDEN GONDOLA
A HAZARD OF HEARTS
A HEART IS BROKEN
THE HIDDEN HEART
THE HORIZONS OF LOVE
IN THE ARMS OF LOVE

THE IRRESISTIBLE BUCK
THE KISS OF PARIS
THE KISS OF THE DEVIL
A KISS OF SILK
THE KNAVE OF HEARTS
THE LEAPING FLAME
A LIGHT TO THE HEART
LIGHTS OF LOVE
THE LITTLE PRETENDER
LOST ENCHANTMENT
LOVE AT FORTY
LOVE FORBIDDEN
LOVE IN HIDING
LOVE IS THE ENEMY
LOVE ME FOREVER
LOVE TO THE RESCUE
LOVE UNDER FIRE
THE MAGIC OF HONEY
METTERNICH THE
    PASSIONATE DIPLOMAT
MONEY, MAGIC AND
    MARRIAGE
NO HEART IS FREE
THE ODIOUS DUKE

OPEN WINGS
A RAINBOW TO HEAVEN
THE RELUCTANT BRIDE
THE SCANDALOUS LIFE
    OF KING CAROL
THE SECRET FEAR
THE SMUGGLED
    HEART
A SONG OF LOVE
STARS IN MY HEART
STOLEN HALO
SWEET ENCHANTRESS
SWEET PUNISHMENT
THEFT OF A HEART
THE THIEF OF LOVE
THIS TIME IT'S LOVE
TOUCH A STAR
TOWARDS THE STARS
THE UNKNOWN HEART
WE DANCED ALL NIGHT
THE WINGS OF ECSTASY
THE WINGS OF LOVE
WINGS ON MY HEART
WOMAN, THE ENIGMA

A NEW CAMFIELD NOVEL OF LOVE BY

BARBARA CARTLAND

Little Tongues of Fire

JOVE BOOKS, NEW YORK

LITTLE TONGUES OF FIRE

A Jove Book/published by arrangement with
the author

PRINTING HISTORY
Jove edition/December 1988

ISBN: 0-515-09843-4

Jove Books are published by The Berkley Publishing Group,
200 Madison Avenue, New York, New York 10016.
The name "JOVE" and the "J" logo
are trademarks belonging to Jove Publications, Inc.

PRINTED IN THE UNITED STATES OF AMERICA

10 9 8 7 6 5 4 3 2 1

Author's Note

IN 1870 the British invented submarine cables and laid one via Gibraltar, Malta, Alexandria, Suez, and Aden to Bombay.

Keeping them open, the safety and the privacy of these lines gave much anxiety. It was one of the great technical tasks of the Empire.

It was a miracle that Britain could keep in touch with the homeland, and with the opening of the Suez Canal it meant that India was not at the other end of the world, but only seventeen days by sea, and four shillings a word standard rate by cable.

By 1890, the Empire was empassed by cables, and the Colonial Office telegraph bill had risen from eight hundred pounds a year, to eight thousand.

chapter one

1875

"I am damned if I will marry anyone!" Lord Edgar Quary said furiously.

He jumped up as he spoke, and walked to the window to stand with his back to the room.

There was silence until the Duke said:

"The alternative . . . is not very attractive."

"What is it?" Lord Edgar asked.

"If you will not marry as I have suggested, the only thing I will do is pay your bills for the last and final time, which is what I said before, on condition that you live abroad."

The Duke paused before he went on:

"I will give you a thousand a year as long as you never come back to England."

There was silence, a silence that seemed somehow to vibrate between the two brothers.

Then Lord Edgar said:

"That is, of course, impossible and intolerable, as you well know!"

"Then I advise you," the Duke said quietly, "to marry Miss Wallace, who has just inherited a fortune of well over a million pounds."

His younger brother did not speak, and the Duke continued:

"It is quite an exciting and unusual story, if you are interested."

There was still silence from Lord Edgar, and the Duke, seeing that he was prepared to listen, said:

"The girl's father, Colonel Wallace, who served as a soldier in India for twenty years before he was killed on the North-West Frontier, apparently saved the Maharajah of Kulhapur's life."

As if he could not help himself from listening to what he was being told, Lord Edgar turned round and in a disdainful manner sat down on the window-seat.

"The Maharajah," his brother went on, "was so grateful that when he died about four months ago, he left Colonel Wallace, who was apparently unaware that he was dead, part of his immense fortune and, I believe, some exceptional jewels."

He paused and looked across the room at Lord Edgar and, because he thought he appeared to be interested, he remarked in a dry, cynical tone:

"It will undoubtedly take you some time to spend all that amount!"

There was an expression of fury on Edgar's handsome face, and he clenched his fists as if he longed to strike his brother.

Instead, he said bitingly:

"You have it all nicely tied up, have you not, Alveric? I should have thought, with all your pompous appreciation of the family tree, that you would resent having it sullied by what is obviously a family of plebeian snobs."

He spoke in a rude and insulting way, but the Duke's expression did not change.

There had been a look of contempt in his grey eyes ever since his brother had arrived from London for an interview which was bound to be unpleasant for both of them.

Now the cynical lines on his face seemed to deepen as he said:

"If that really perturbs you, it will gratify you to know that the Wallaces are an old Scottish family who have attained distinction generation after generation in the Army."

"I suppose I should be pleased about that!" Lord Edgar said, still in a rude tone of voice.

"General Sir Alexander Wallace," the Duke continued, "has received a number of medals for bravery in combat and was, I am told, much respected by his Regiment and is well spoken of in the County."

"Does he want my title for his niece," Lord Edgar snapped, "or is it Miss Wallace's ambition to be affiliated to a Duke?"

"I think," the Duke replied, "that the idea came from the girl's aunt, who is the General's second wife and much younger than he. As you say, it will be an advantage to them all to be affiliated to the Dukedom of Quarington."

Lord Edgar laughed. It was not a particularly pleasant sound.

"So, to achieve a position in the highest Society, they

are prepared to accept the black sheep of the family, who, of course, is me!"

The Duke rose and stood with his back to the fire-place.

He was a very good-looking man. The two brothers would have been outstanding in any gathering, even if no one had known who they were.

The Duke was a few inches taller than his brother and, although he habitually looked bored and cynical, it did not detract from his appearance in the same way as did the lines of debauchery on Lord Edgar's face.

They were just beginning to appear, even though he was three years younger than the Duke.

The life he lived in London had made him less ath-letic than his brother, and his waistline was considerably larger.

The Quarys were known for their handsome men, and ambitious Mamas had tried for years to ensnare the head of the family.

The Duke had, however, stated a long time ago that he had no intention of marrying and, at thirty-four, was adroit enough to avoid every type of bait and trap that was set for him.

He was, nevertheless, very conscious of his responsi-bilities as head of one of the most respected families in the Kingdom.

He had struggled for years to try to force his younger brother to curb his extravagance and refrain from adding to his already raffish reputation.

But Lord Edgar would listen to no-one.

He led a life of wild and unrestrained luxury, giving parties that were the delight of every sponger and "soiled dove" in the whole of London.

He raced horses which never won and lost astronomical amounts on ridiculous bets. His behaviour caused amusement and speculation in the Clubs of St. James's.

However, when the Duke was presented with the bills, he knew he could not go on forever financing his brother's spendthrift ways.

He had said repeatedly:

"I am responsible not only for you, Edgar, but for every member of our family."

"And how you enjoy it!" Lord Edgar said sarcastically.

"It is not particularly enjoyable to see our Almshouses falling into disrepair, our Schools needing more teachers, our Clergymen complaining that their stipends are too low, and our relations being put on 'short commons'—just to finance you!"

"By God, Alveric," Lord Edgar ejaculated, "you talk as if you were down to your last penny. You know as well as I do that you are a very rich man with treasures in every house you possess."

"Treasures which are only in trust for the generations that come after me."

"Are you worrying about the son you do not have?" Lord Edgar asked mockingly.

The Duke did not deign to answer.

He knew his brother was well aware that the pictures and furniture were all entailed for his successors just as they had been for him when he inherited.

He had paid thousands upon thousands of pounds during the last few years to his brother's creditors and he had known for some time that eventually there must be a curb to his extravagance.

The opportunity had come quite unexpectedly.

To the Duke's surprise, General Sir Alexander Wallace and his wife had called on him one day after he had arrived home from London.

Although he had met the General on one or two formal occasions, the Wallaces were not on the list of neighbours whom he invited to his dinner parties.

Nor did they attend the intimate gatherings which took place frequently at his ancestral home.

He supposed, although he was not sure, that they were included in the garden party which he traditionally gave every year, just as his father and his grandfather had done before him.

At these parties there was a large Marquee on one of the lawns and a Band playing, while the guests wandered round the terraces admiring the water garden, some playing bowls on the Bowling Green.

Some would spend an hour or so drawing a bow, for archery butts were always in evidence.

The Duke would welcome his guests, and then stroll among the crowd talking to this person and that.

He was often uncertain of their names or if he had ever met them before.

He had, of course, agreed to see the General when he was told that he and his wife were at the front door.

When they were shown into the Drawing-Room, he wondered if they had come to solicit his help for some charity in which he was not already engaged.

There was a great many of these. His secretary had a long list of those to which he contributed generously each year.

He thought after he had shaken hands with the General that he looked his age and that he seemed slightly embarrassed.

His second wife, however, seemed very much at her ease and cast the Duke the admiring and flirtatious glances to which he was well accustomed.

They sat down, the Duke offering them some refreshment which they refused.

Then, after an awkward silence, the General cleared his throat and began:

"Your Grace must be a little surprised to see us, and perhaps what we have to say may come as an even greater surprise."

The Duke inclined his head but did not speak. The General went on:

"I have heard from a number of sources which I need not disclose that your brother, Lord Edgar, is in some financial difficulty."

The Duke stiffened.

He resented an outsider speaking of what he thought should be an entirely family affair.

He could only wonder how it was possible that Edgar, unpredictable though he was, should owe money to the General.

"I have heard, in fact," the General went on, "that Lord Edgar is talking of disposing of his horses and that several pictures of family interest are up for sale at Christie's."

The Duke's lips tightened.

He thought furiously that if Edgar were selling any pictures, they were not his, but belonged to the family collection. He had only been lent them for his house in London.

The General had stopped speaking and the Duke said in a voice that was deliberately aloof and cold:

"You, General, are obviously better informed than I

am about my brother, but I will, of course, make enquiries to find out if what you tell me is correct."

"I do not think you will discover that I have misled Your Grace," the General said. "My wife, however, has a solution to Lord Edgar's problem."

The Duke raised his eyebrows.

Then, as if she could not remain silent any longer, Lady Wallace said:

"It seems so sad that anyone so handsome as Lord Edgar should be in such dire straits. My friend, Lady Farringham, whom I think you know, tells me she is really sorry for the poor young man not knowing where the next penny is coming from."

It was with the greatest difficulty that the Duke repressed a desire to tell Lady Wallace to mind her own business.

But only four months before he had paid his brother's debts which had amounted to nearly thirty thousand pounds.

Then Edgar had sworn to him by everything he held sacred that he would be more careful in future.

"What my husband and I would like to suggest," Lady Wallace went on, "would not only be of assistance to Your Grace, but also to ourselves."

The Duke looked puzzled, and she said:

"I suppose you have heard of my husband's brother, Colonel David Wallace, who was awarded the Distinguished Service Order for his brilliant exploits in India before he was killed on the North-West Frontier?"

"Yes, I have, of course, heard of him," the Duke replied.

He was not particularly interested. He thought, however, it was the only polite thing to say.

"Well, apparently," Lady Wallace went on, "my brother-in-law in some skirmish or other, which they always appear to be having in India, saved the life of the Maharajah of Kulhapur. He did not tell us anything about it at the time, but three months ago the Maharajah died."

The Duke, wondering what all this had to do with him or Edgar, forced himself to look attentive.

"You can imagine our astonishment," Lady Wallace continued, "when we learned that my husband's niece, Vina, who is our ward and has been living with us since her father's death, has now inherited such an enormous sum of money. It should have gone to her father had he been alive. We can hardly credit that we are not dreaming!"

Lady Wallace paused for breath, and the General interjected:

"The Maharajah was one of the richest men in India. He left my brother well over a million pounds, and jewellery which might have come from an Aladdin's Cave."

"You are certainly to be congratulated," the Duke said politely.

"What we thought," Lady Wallace said a little nervously, "is that Vina, who is a very pretty young girl, might, if Your Grace agrees, marry Lord Edgar."

The Duke looked at Lady Wallace in astonishment, as if he thought he had not heard her right.

Then, as the silence was uncomfortable, he asked:

"Are you suggesting . . . ?"

"You must see," Lady Wallace interrupted, "that it would save us worrying about fortune hunters who will certainly pursue Vina once the extent of her fortune was

9

known, and would also relieve Lord Edgar of seeking assistance from Your Grace."

The way she spoke told the Duke quite clearly that his brother's frequent pleas for money had not gone unnoticed by the County.

Lord Edgar's financial straits were well known in London, where gossip flew on the wind, but he had not suspected his difficulties were common knowledge locally.

At the same time, he saw exactly what the General and Lady Wallace were offering him, and, as they had said, it certainly seemed a solution to the problem.

"Has your niece met my brother?" he asked the General.

Lady Wallace answered for her husband.

"No, of course not. Vina was in mourning until the beginning of this year. We were planning, my husband and I, to take her to London next month so that she could make her curtsy at Buckingham Palace and become a *débutante*. We were even thinking we might afford to give a small Ball for her."

She glanced at the General as she spoke, and the Duke was aware that she was looking forward to a Ball and any other entertainments which might take place in London.

She would doubtless appreciate them, he thought, even more than her niece.

"How old is Miss Vina Wallace?" the Duke asked.

"She is eighteen."

"And you consider her a suitable wife for my brother, who will be thirty-two in July?"

"I think any girl would be very lucky, Your Grace, to marry into your family."

That, the Duke thought, was the crux of the whole matter!

Of course the General and Lady Wallace wanted to be affiliated to the Quarys, for to be *persona grata* with their relations, all of whom had married into the most respected families in the land, would be a great social accolade.

For a moment the Duke longed to tell them that the Quary name was not for sale and that they could take their money elsewhere.

Then he wondered if, perhaps, this might not be the saving of Edgar.

If he had a wife, there was just a chance, although it was a very long shot, that he might settle down and behave better than he was doing at the moment.

When the Duke thought of the immense amount of money Edgar had been spending on what were called "soiled doves"—actresses, ballet dancers—and on the jewels for which they all apparently had an insatiable desire, it made him furious.

It seemed impossible that any man could run through so much money in so short a time.

He guessed that the only reason that Edgar had not been back begging him once again to pay his debts was that he had made so great a scene four months before.

It was obviously something his brother, like himself, wished to avoid for as long as possible.

Perhaps this might be the answer.

He was not sure, but it seemed at least better than making further economies in his own affairs as he had had to before Christmas, when Edgar had demanded thirty thousand pounds, and got it.

"May I say," he replied to Lady Wallace, "that I

would like to think over your proposition, and, of course, discuss it with my brother. I can only thank you both for making such a suggestion. I hope I shall be able to give you an answer in the very near future."

He rose to his feet as he spoke.

There was nothing the General and Lady Wallace could do but rise too.

The Duke thanked them again for coming and escorted them to the front door.

Their carriage was waiting, and, as they walked down the steps, it was with difficulty, as Lady Wallace looked back and waved her hand, that the Duke forced a smile to his lips.

Then he walked to his Study in a black rage, which made him long to strike somebody, preferably Edgar.

How was it possible, how was it believable that he could have got himself into the same mess he had been in half a dozen times before, and in less than six months?

Another man might have sworn aloud in his rage, or at least taken a strong drink from the tantalus table which stood in a corner of the room.

But the Duke only walked to the window to stare out with unseeing eyes at the garden, where the first spring flowers were just coming into bloom.

He was thinking of how he had tried ever since his parents' death to look after Edgar.

He had, however, failed in his attempts to make him behave in what to him was an ordinary and normal manner.

But Edgar had laughed at everything that was respectable.

He disliked most of the people who wished to be friendly for the sake of the family.

He had made himself the leader of what was a raffish and ill-behaved, drunken crowd of young men, already notorious for their behaviour in London and the country.

They had drunk and broken up the Nightclubs where they spent most of their evenings.

They had arranged Steeple-Chases where the competitors were usually so drunk that they had become involved in a series of accidents.

What was more, the Duke had already been reprimanded by the Queen for allowing his brother to run riot in such a disreputable manner.

"What can I do? Where have I failed?" he had asked himself a hundred times, and not yet found an answer.

As his anger gradually subsided, he told himself that perhaps this was indeed a chance not to be missed.

If Miss Vina Wallace was prepared to sell herself for a title, then she must be a tough young woman who could undoubtedly cope with Edgar and his peculiarities.

He thought things over for some time, then rang the bell for his Secretary.

John Simpson had served with the Duke in the Horse Guards.

When, on inheriting the title, the Duke left, he had asked Simpson to come with him as Secretary, or what was known in Royal Circles as Comptroller, for he knew he was a most able man.

Simpson, who could not afford the Horse Guards, although his father had served in it, jumped at the opportunity.

He liked the Duke and admired him enormously.

Such a solution would solve his financial worries.

He took the running of Quarington over from a much older man and brought it to as near perfection as was possible.

Because he was a gentleman, the old servants who had been there for years liked him. They did not resent him tactfully suggesting new methods which they would have instinctively fought against had they come from anybody else.

Now as John Simpson, who was getting on towards forty, came into the room, the Duke said:

"General Wallace and his wife have just called on me."

"I was aware of that, Your Grace."

"You will hardly believe why they came!"

There was a mischievous twinkle in John Simpson's eye as he replied:

"I think, Your Grace, that it concerned Lord Edgar."

The Duke sat upright.

"How on earth can you know that?"

"Even the bees carry news in this County, from flower to flower!" John Simpson said. "And I heard two weeks ago that Miss Vina Wallace had inherited a fortune."

"So you knew they would be suggesting that she should marry Lord Edgar?"

"Lady Wallace has always been extremely ambitious to move in the same set as Your Grace!"

The Duke could not help laughing.

"I cannot believe it, John. If you know all this, why did you not tell me?"

"I did not think about it until I learned that the General and Lady Wallace had been here and I guessed they had actually been brave enough to approach you."

"But you knew they were thinking about it?"

"I was told by some mutual friends about a fortnight ago," John Simpson replied, "what was Lady Wallace's greatest ambition, and that she had Lord Edgar in mind."

"What has he been up to now?" the Duke asked.

"He has lost a great deal of money on the race-course," Simpson replied, "and he has also taken under his protection the most expensive young woman from the Olympic Theatre. Her carriage, horses, and jewels are the envy of everybody else in her profession."

The Duke was still for a moment. Then he said:

"If he wants to live like a Maharajah, it is only poetic justice that he should spend a Maharajah's money! Send for him, John, and say I wish to speak to him."

Looking at his brother now, the Duke supposed that, as he was so good-looking, any woman would find it easy to forgive him his sins.

But he could not help thinking that Miss Wallace would need an iron determination and unusual total in-sensitivity to cope with anyone who was so profligate where money was concerned.

As if he knew what his brother was thinking, Lord Edgar said:

"I suppose it is something I shall have to accept, but you had better give me a house where I can leave the blasted woman while I enjoy myself in London!"

"If she has any sense, she will tie up her money so that she can limit the amount you can spend," the Duke remarked.

"In which case, I will not marry her!" Lord Edgar replied.

"I have already pointed out that you really have no choice," the Duke retorted.

"Well, do not make things any more difficult for me than they are already," Lord Edgar snapped. "If she wants my title, that is what she shall have. I want her fortune, but I am not having it doled out like a schoolboy's pocket money!"

"That, of course, is up to you," the Duke said, "and I suppose the first step, if we are to behave correctly, is to ask the Wallaces to stay, and for you to meet Miss Vina while she is festooned in the jewels which are part of the package!"

There was no mistaking the contempt in the Duke's voice, and Lord Edgar said:

"There is no point in being nasty about it, Alveric; at least *you* are 'off the hook.'"

"That is true if a somewhat vulgar way of putting it," the Duke agreed.

"Well then, stop bellyaching and let us get on with it. There are one or two people who have to be paid immediately. I suppose you would not care to advance me five thousand pounds?"

"I would not!" the Duke said firmly.

"Very well then," Lord Edgar said, "the sooner the marriage takes place the better! Which house are you going to give me?"

The Duke thought for a moment. Then he said:

"The Dower House, I suppose."

"That will do," Lord Edgar agreed. "At least it is large enough to entertain in, and, of course, we can always come here."

He glanced at his brother as if for confirmation, and the Duke said:

"I will be delighted to welcome your guests so long as they are approved by your wife."

"I thought perhaps you would like to meet Connie," Lord Edgar jeered.

"If Connie is the woman who has got you into the mess you are in now," the Duke replied, "I hope you will have the good sense and, of course, the decency to give her up."

"You must think I am crazy!" Lord Edgar exclaimed. "Connie is without exception the most amusing and quite the most exotic 'Charmer' I have met for a long time. I grant you she is expensive, but she is worth every penny."

"I can only hope your future wife will think so," the Duke said coldly.

He walked to the door, then looked back, saying:

"As we do not want it to appear as though you are rushing to get your hands on the Maharajah's rupees, may I suggest that I ask the Wallaces and their niece to come here from next Friday until Monday, and I will invite a few of my more *respectable* friends to meet them."

He accentuated the word "respectable" and Lord Edgar laughed mockingly.

"In which case it will be crashingly dull," he said, "and I shall return to Connie on Monday morning—as early as possible!"

The Duke was about to make some retort but decided it would be undignified.

Instead, he went out of the room, shutting the door quietly behind him.

He was aware, as he walked down the corridor, that his brother was laughing.

The Butler proffered Lady Wallace a letter and, as she took it from the silver salver, she asked:

"Who is it from, Barlow?"

"It's just been delivered, M'Lady, by a groom from Quarington."

Lady Wallace gave a start. There was a sudden glint in her eye as she carried the note to the writing-table and slit it open.

She read its contents carefully and gave a little cry of delight.

Then she ran down the passage to where her husband was sitting in his Study, reading the *Morning Post*.

She burst into the room and ran to his chair, saying:

"He has agreed! Alexander, he has agreed!"

The General put down the *Morning Post* and looked up at his wife.

"Are you speaking of the Duke?" he asked.

"Yes, of course! He has agreed to what we suggested and has asked us to come and stay next Friday at Quarington!"

She gave another cry and said:

"I can hardly believe it! Oh, Alexander, we shall be able to go frequently to that wonderful house, and, of course, meet the Duke's friends!"

"I am surprised that Quarington agreed," the General said slowly. "In fact, I was convinced he would refuse us categorically and without making any excuses."

"I told you that Lord Edgar was desperate. In fact, Edith Farringham said that her husband had told her he owes nearly fifty thousand pounds!"

"Stupid young fool! Why does he want to throw

away money he has not got?" the General asked.

"He will have it now, and Vina will be Lady Edgar Quary! Think of it, Alexander, she will have the *entrée* to Court Circles, and you may be quite certain we shall be asked to all the houses that have looked down their noses at us up until now."

The General was not listening.

He was reading the newspaper again and paid no attention as his wife stood reading again the Duke's note. She thought how aristocratic his handwriting was.

"I am sure," she continued, "when we are in London we will sooner or later be invited to Devonshire House."

Her voice had a rapt note in it and, as if suddenly aware that his wife was still speaking, the General looked over his newspaper at her to ask:

"Have you told Vina?"

"Told her what?"

"That she is to marry Edgar Quary?"

"No, of course not! I did not wish to talk about it until it was a *fait accompli*. She is a very, very lucky girl, as I hope she will realise."

"You had better break it to her gently. After all, it is she who has to marry him, not you."

"Really, Alexander, you do say the most ridiculous things! Young girls, as you well know, marry whom they are told to by their Guardians, and I hope one day Vina will thank us for all the trouble we have taken over her."

Now there was a slightly plaintive note in the way Lady Wallace spoke, as if she realised that Vina would not be as grateful as she had at first expected.

Then she asked:

"Will you tell her, or shall I?"

19

"As it was your idea in the first place," the General replied, "I think it had better come from you. I confess I am very surprised that Quary, who is very conscious of his own importance, has agreed."

"Of course he has agreed!" Lady Wallace said positively. "How could he do anything else?"

As he did not wish to be involved in an argument, the General went back to reading his newspaper.

Lady Wallace looked at the Duke's letter again; then, going from the Study she walked into the hall.

"Do you know where Miss Vina is?" she asked the Butler, who was tidying away the riding whips which lay on a table under the stairs.

"She is in the Library, M'Lady."

"I might have guessed that!" Lady Wallace said with asperity, and walked to the Library, which was a somewhat bleak room to which she and the General rarely went.

It was, nevertheless, lined with books, most of which had been inherited from the General's father.

Lady Wallace had no time for reading, except, of course, for the *Ladies Journal* and the Court Circulars in the newspapers.

It had surprised her to find that her husband's niece was content to sit hour after hour reading.

What was more, since she had returned to England, Vina had spent quite a considerable amount of her money on books.

She was sitting now in the window, curled up in what Lady Wallace thought was a slightly unladylike manner. She was so intent on what she was reading that she did not hear her aunt approach her.

"Vina!" Lady Wallace ejaculated.

Her niece looked up with a smile.

"Did you want me, Aunt Marjory?"

"I cannot think what you are doing in here on such a lovely morning, when you could be out in the garden."

"I went riding before breakfast," Vina replied, "and I was wondering whether Uncle Alexander would ride with me after luncheon."

"You must ask him," Lady Wallace said vaguely. "Now, listen, Vina, I have something to tell you which I know you might find very exciting."

Vina's large eyes were fixed dutifully on her aunt's face.

Yet Lady Wallace had the impression that her thoughts were still with the book she had been reading.

"Listen," she said again, "we have been asked by the Duke of Quarington to stay with him next Friday!"

She waited for Vina's cry of delight, but the girl only looked at her, asking in a puzzled voice:

"Have I met the Duke?"

"No, of course not!" Lady Wallace replied. "You would remember it if you had. He is very handsome— and very important."

"And you are pleased that we have been asked to stay?" Vina said, trying to fathom why they had been invited.

"Of course I am pleased!" Lady Wallace replied. "And so should you be. It is a very great privilege to stay at Quarington, which is without exception one of the most magnificent houses in England."

"Then I should like to see it," Vina said, "and I expect they have a large Library."

"I am sure it is enormous!" Lady Wallace said vaguely. "But what is important, Vina, is that you are to meet the Duke's brother, Lord Edgar Quary."

Vina waited as if there should be further explanation, and Lady Wallace went on:

"I am sure he will be attracted to you, and you by him. He is very handsome."

"What does he do?" Vina asked.

"Do?" her aunt repeated. "What do you mean by that?"

"I mean is he a soldier . . . or a Member of Parliament?"

"He is neither!" Lady Wallace said sharply. "The Duke was a soldier for some years, but everyone is not like your father and your uncle, always wanting to order people about—or kill them!"

"I know Papa would never have killed anybody unless they had shot at him first," Vina replied quickly.

"I am not concerned with your father at the moment," Lady Wallace said. "We are talking about Lord Edgar. I want you to be very charming to him, and, of course, very polite to the Duke, who is the head of the family."

"Are they important to Uncle Alexander?"

"Yes, of course they are!" Lady Wallace replied. "And important to you too."

"To me?"

The surprise in Vina's voice made Lady Wallace hesitate before she said any more.

Perhaps it would be better, she thought, if Vina met Lord Edgar without being self-conscious and shy.

It was something she would undoubtedly be if she knew she was expected to marry a man she had never seen.

Therefore, with a smile, Lady Wallace said:

"What you and I have to do now, Vina, is to see that we have enough clothes to look smart, very smart, when we go to Quarington. Neither of us wants to be outshone or look like country bumpkins!"

Vina laughed.

"You could never look like that, Aunt Marjory!"

"And you also have to look your best," Lady Wallace said, "so we had better slip up to London to-morrow and buy ourselves some really wonderful gowns in Bond Street."

Vina closed the book and put it down.

Ever since she had come to England she had realised that the one thing her aunt really enjoyed was shopping.

It was something she herself found rather irksome unless she could contrive to get to a bookshop.

But because she was sensitive, she realised from her aunt's voice that this visit to which they had been invited was important.

"I will make all the arrangements," Lady Wallace was saying, "and, if we leave early, we should be in London by about noon."

"Very well, Aunt Marjory," Vina replied.

She thought her aunt was looking at her in a rather strange manner, but then, as Lady Wallace turned away, she told herself she was imagining things.

"Clothes, more clothes!" she said to herself, and added: "Oh, Papa, if only you were here, everything would be so different."

She had a sudden longing for India, for the heat, the slow-moving bare-footed servants, the *punkahs* swaying overhead, and the creak of the water wheel outside.

It would be a very unkind thing to say that she found

England dull, for her uncle and aunt had been so good to her.

She longed for the men who had always been dropping in to see her father when she had been looking after him after her mother had died.

She loved the lessons that she had had from a Schoolmaster, a retired Professor and an Indian, who had been to England and had a Cambridge degree.

There was so much to learn, so much to hear, so much to feel.

Then she told herself she was being very ungrateful and it was simply that the transition from one life to another had made her feel lost and lonely.

There was nobody she could talk to as she had been able to talk to her father and his Indian friends.

"Oh, Papa," she cried in her heart, "why did you have to die and leave me alone?"

Then, as if in answer to her question, she could see his face smiling at her.

His eyes seemed to twinkle as when they were engaged in a spirited argument which had kept them talking from the beginning of a meal to the end.

"I am not really alone," she told herself.

She tried to talk to her father as she would have done had he been beside her.

chapter two

THE Duke had chosen his house-party with much care.

He thought it would be a great mistake for it to be too small, worse for it to be too big.

He also wanted to invite people who would not be particularly interested in what Edgar was doing so that he would have a chance to get to know Miss Wallace.

As he was thinking of his own amusement, too, he included Lady Irene Halford, whom he knew would be only too eager to accept his invitation.

He had realised for some time that Lady Irene was stalking him, as he described it privately to himself, and was not certain whether or not he would succumb to her blandishments, which were very obvious.

At the same time, she was one of the most beautiful women in London.

Her classical features and perfectly proportioned

body had attracted his attention the first time he had seen her.

Her husband, Lord Halford, was at least twenty years older than his wife.

He was, therefore, more concerned with his duties at Court than with escorting her to all the Balls and Receptions to which they were invited.

The Duke was, therefore, well aware that if he accepted her attentions, in Lady Irene's eyes he would be hurting no-one, and there would certainly be no scandal.

He would not be the first lover she had taken.

But she behaved in so circumspect a manner that even the gossips found it difficult to say anything unpleasant about her.

As he expected, Lady Irene answered his invitation by return.

The Duke also included a few of his own particular men friends, who always made a success of any party he gave.

He thought he would invite some neighbors to dinner on the Saturday evening, then see how the party progressed before he planned what they would do on Sunday.

The Duke discussed it all with John Simpson.

He arranged everything in the household—servants, Chefs, and the bedroom plans, leaving the Duke to cope with his brother.

"I suppose," Lord Edgar said sourly at breakfast on Friday morning, "that you expect me to make myself pleasant to this title-seeking country bumpkin you have chosen as my future wife?"

The Duke did not reply, and Lord Edgar, pushing his

plate away from him disdainfully as if he were not hungry, said:

"The more I think of it, the more I am inclined to go abroad. I seem to remember that was the alternative."

"There is nothing to stop you," the Duke answered, "but I think you would miss your horses, your friends, your Clubs, and the fact that, being English, wherever you live you would always be a foreigner."

"I would find that an advantage!" Lord Edgar retorted truculently.

"Then, of course, it is quite easy for you not to propose to Miss Wallace over the week-end. Let me know to which foreign Bank I am to send your allowance."

"Dammit all, Alveric," Lord Edgar shouted. "I *am* your brother, and as it happens, I am also your heir apparent, as you have no son."

For a moment the Duke was still. Then he said, almost as if he were speaking to himself:

"I had forgotten that!"

"Well, it is true," Lord Edgar said, "and if you want to know, I have already approached the Usurers to see what they will advance me on the chance of my succeeding on your death."

"You have done what?" the Duke asked angrily.

"You heard what I said," Lord Edgar answered, "but actually, the old skinflints were not interested. They said you are too young for there to be any reason for your dying *normally*."

He accentuated the word "normally," and the Duke remarked:

"Perhaps you are thinking of some clever way of disposing of me without being brought to justice?"

"I am not such a fool as to risk being hanged," Lord

27

Edgar retorted, "but if you did happen to break your neck out riding, or drown in the lake, it would certainly solve my problems!"

The idea of Lord Edgar taking his place was so unpleasant that the Duke returned to reading the newspaper which was propped up in front of him on a silver stand.

"Supposing that this girl," Edgar began in a low voice, "is as plain as a pikestaff and speaks to me as her father did to the raw recruits he had under his command?"

He sounded so depressed that the Duke could not help smiling as he replied:

"In which case you can always look for another heiress, but those as rich as Miss Wallace are few and far between."

"Perhaps the stories of her fortune are exaggerated," Lord Edgar suggested. "What do we do then?"

"I cannot think that the General, who is quite obviously a straight-forward and honest man, would lie," the Duke answered.

Lord Edgar rose from the table, pushing back his chair violently.

"Well, I might as well enjoy my last hours of freedom," he said. "I suppose it is too late for me to slip up to London and see Connie before these title-seekers arrive?"

The Duke thought it was beneath his dignity to answer.

He continued reading the newspaper as his brother gave an exasperated sound that was half an oath and went out of the room, slamming the door behind him.

The Duke sighed and, sitting back in his chair, wondered for the thousandth time how he had managed to fail with Edgar.

He had been such an attractive little boy.

Yet, looking back, the Duke knew that even when they were very small, Edgar had resented him because he was more important than himself.

From the moment he was grown up Edgar had done everything he could, not only to disparage his elder brother, but also to draw attention to himself.

The Duke supposed that psychologically the reason that Edgar behaved in such an outrageous manner, and had done so ever since he had been at Eton, was because he wanted to inherit the Dukedom.

As the Duke had gradually come to realise this, he had gone out of his way to do more for Edgar than anyone else would have done in similar circumstances.

Even the family Solicitors and the Trustees of the estate had remonstrated with him.

They told him he was giving his brother far too much money, and in consequence denying others who were more worthy of his help.

Lord Edgar had showed no gratitude but seemed determined to provoke not only the Duke but his whole family.

It made the Duke more cynical than ever.

When he was young he had been very badly treated by the first woman with whom he fell in love.

His father had been alive and in good health, and there had seemed then little chance of Alveric inheriting the title for at least twenty years.

While the young woman had encouraged the Duke's advances, she had not really considered him seriously.

Because she was very beautiful, and in many ways

sophisticated, he had been head over heels in love with her.

It had, therefore, been a cruel shock when he learned that she was laughing at him behind his back.

She even read aloud to her intimate friends, who considered the Duke a joke, the letters he wrote her.

Because he was extremely sensitive, the hurt she inflicted on him took a long time to heal.

But although he appeared to have recovered, the scars remained.

What was more, when the 5th Duke died unexpectedly from appendicitis and Alveric inherited, the girl he had loved realised what a mistake she had made.

Throwing over the man to whom she had become engaged, she tried to revive the love she had so cruelly thrown away.

It was perhaps this more than anything else which had made the Duke decide that all women were treacherous and that he had no wish to marry.

He would not have been human if he had not accepted the favours he was offered.

Yet he was convinced that when women expressed their love for him, they were thinking of his coronet and not of him as a man.

The lines of cynicism on his face deepened as he told himself that never again would he look at, or be interested in, a young, unmarried woman.

He was involved only with the sophisticated beauties who deceived their husbands cleverly enough to avoid any scandal.

They hid their fiery desires in public, but privately most men found them irresistible.

The Duke could pick and choose, and every year he became more fastidious.

It became a feather in a woman's cap when it was whispered that the Duke was her lover.

Even so, the women he chose never knew from one meeting to the next if the Duke was, as she longed for, as infatuated with her as she was with him.

The Duke thought as he left the Breakfast Room that there was nothing more he could do for his brother.

The sooner Lady Irene arrived and his thoughts could be elsewhere, the better.

It was John Simpson who knew more than anybody else what his master was feeling, and he reminded himself that what he wanted was the Duke's happiness.

It seemed extraordinary, with all his great possessions and surrounded by those who admired him, that he could not be happy.

And yet, John Simpson was aware that in fact the Duke was a lonely man.

There was a great deal missing in his life which could not be purchased with money.

It was a feeling he would not put into words.

Looking over his guest list, he found himself hoping that when Lord Edgar married Miss Wallace, he would improve his way of life.

Perhaps in that way the Duke would have one burden less on his shoulders.

* * *

Vina was feeling somewhat bewildered as she drove with her uncle and aunt towards Quarington.

Even with the knowledge that, apparently, her aunt Marjory's idea of Paradise was to be the guest of the

Duke, she could not account for the fact that her uncle appeared to be somewhat uneasy.

She had the feeling, although she had nothing to substantiate it, that where she was concerned he was slightly embarrassed.

She thought of the magnificent Palaces she had visited in India with her father, and could not imagine that Quarington would be any more awe-inspiring than they were.

Or, she mused, that the Duke could be more terrifying than some of the elderly Indian Princes.

Lady Wallace had been fussing about Vina's clothes, her packing, and her hair even before breakfast and had continued giving orders and counter-orders all through the day.

When finally, at four o'clock in the afternoon, they set off towards Quarington, Vina was quite exhausted by her aunt's excitement.

She also had to listen to long and, to her, boring discussions as to what she should wear.

The gowns that they had bought in Bond Street were certainly very attractive.

As money was of no consequence where Vina was concerned, her aunt had automatically ordered the most expensive.

Fortunately, Lady Wallace had very good taste, and she did not make the mistake of dressing Vina too elaborately.

At the same time, she expected perfection and complained noisily if she thought she was not getting it.

She changed her mind no less than four times on what Vina should wear to arrive, with the result that the young maid who looked after her was nearly in tears before everything was finally packed.

They set off in the large carriage which, although slightly old-fashioned, was very comfortable.

Vina sat with her back to the horses, opposite her uncle and aunt.

She had the feeling they were looking at her in a strange way.

It was almost as if they were appraising her and had something on their minds that they could not say.

She could not imagine why she had this impression, but it persisted.

As they drove down the drive towards the great house which had been so often described to Vina by her aunt that she felt she knew it already, Lady Wallace exclaimed:

"We are here, and what could be more exciting? Put your bonnet straight, Vina, and shake out your skirts as soon as you step from the carriage. I do not want you to look creased."

"Yes, Aunt Marjory," Vina agreed meekly.

She was thinking, craning her neck forward to look at the house as they drove nearer to it, that Quarington was exceedingly impressive and exactly as she had expected it to look.

There was something a little austere about its architectural symmetry which appealed to her, while the green leaves spreading down to the lake, on which there were swans and ducks, were very attractive.

"Could anything be more grand or more beautiful?" Lady Wallace enthused.

They were escorted up the steps, on which had been laid a red carpet, by footmen in the Quarington livery, whose crested buttons glinted in the afternoon sun.

As Vina followed her aunt and uncle towards the front door, she thought they might be the Viceroy and the Vicereine of India, and the idea made her smile.

At the same time, it made her long once again to be back in that country, for she had been so happy there.

A grey-haired Butler, looking like an Archbishop, escorted them across the marble floor of the huge hall where ancient flags flew above a curved marble mantelpiece.

They recorded the battles in which the Duke's ancestors had fought.

Vina knew that her father would have been interested in them.

She was thinking as they entered the Drawing-Room of the many battles in which he had been engaged.

He had survived death dozens of times, finally to die from a mere skirmish with the tribesmen on the North-West Frontier.

'If only I could have talked to him for one moment before he died,' Vina thought.

She recalled the agony of how she felt when she learned he was dead and forgot for a moment where she was.

It was, therefore, with a start that she heard her uncle say:

"Your Grace, may I present my niece, Vina."

She realised then that standing in front of her was a tall, exceedingly handsome man whom she knew was the Duke.

He held out his hand and said in a deep voice:

"Welcome to Quarington, Miss Wallace!"

She dropped him a small curtsy and, as she looked

up, the Duke saw the pain in her eyes, which surprised him.

Then they were being introduced to several other guests, but Lord Edgar was not amongst them.

They sat down and talked, Lady Wallace having plenty to say to one of the other ladies present, while the Duke talked to the General about horses.

"I see in the newspapers," the General remarked, "that you had a good win at Newmarket two days ago."

"It pleased me because it was a new horse," the Duke answered, "one I purchased only six months ago. It was doubtful if he would win that particular race."

"Well, you were successful, as you usually are," the General remarked.

"Do you ride, Miss Wallace?" the Duke asked, bringing Vina into the conversation.

"Yes, Your Grace, and I enjoy it very much," Vina replied.

"Then you may like to try out one of my horses to-morrow morning," the Duke said.

"I would love that," Vina replied.

She was thinking, as she spoke, of the thin skittish little horses she had ridden in India.

Very fast, they had been hard to hold, and she had found her uncle's horses rather tame and slow by comparison.

It made her say to the Duke:

"It would be exciting to ride one of your horses, but please, Your Grace, give me one that is not over-trained."

The Duke raised his eyebrows.

"What do you mean by that?"

Vina realised she had spoken without thinking, and,

not wishing to be rude to her uncle, she said:

"I am used to horses that are not especially kept for young ladies who are not sure of their equestrian prowess."

The Duke laughed.

"I know exactly what you mean, and I promise you shall have something fast and spirited."

Vina smiled, and he thought she was not only very attractive but lovely.

She was not in the least what he had expected. He had fancied that the General's niece would be a heavy, countrified girl with fair hair and blue eyes.

Vina's hair was almost dark, and there was strange lights in it.

On the other hand, her eyes had a touch of green in them which was in striking contrast to the whiteness of her skin.

At the same time, her face was young. Yet there was a quality about it that he could not remember having seen before in a girl.

He realised it was perhaps that ageless look that could be found in Greek statues.

Then, as he thought about it, he remembered the drawings he had seen when he was in India.

He remembered that was where Vina's father had died, and asked:

"Were you in India with your father?"

"I was born there and I lived in India until Papa was . . . killed . . . and I had to come . . . to England."

There was a note in her voice, and also a look in her eyes, which told him how much her father had meant to her.

The Duke knew in some strange way that she had

been thinking of India when they had first been introduced.

When the ladies rose to go upstairs to rest and change
before dinner, the Duke became aware of the grace with
which Vina moved.

It reminded him of the way Indian women walked
whilst carrying a burden on their heads.

He found himself watching her as she moved towards
the door, following her aunt, who was still talking animatedly to one of his relations.

Then, as they disappeared, the Duke remembered
that the General was left behind. He sat down beside
him.

"I am sorry my brother is not here to greet you," he
said. "He went out riding soon after luncheon and must
have ridden farther than he intended."

The other men were talking on the other side of the
fireplace, and the Duke lowered his voice as he asked:

"Is your niece, Miss Wallace, looking forward to
meeting my brother?"

The General realised they could not be overheard,
and said in a conspiratorial tone:

"My wife thought it wiser not to tell her that there
was an ulterior motive in our staying this weekend."

The Duke raised his eye-brows.

"You mean she does not know what you have
planned?"

"She has not the slightest idea!"

The Duke was surprised and also a little concerned.

Because Edgar had reiterated many times that Vina
Wallace was after his title, the Duke had almost begun
to believe it was a fair exchange.

Now he found himself wondering, not what Edgar

37

would think of Vina, but what she would think of him.

He had the uncomfortable feeling that she would not change his way of life, as he had hoped, but merely be shocked by it.

* * *

In the luxurious bedroom where her trunk had been unpacked and preparations made for her bath in front of a small fire, Vina was glad to be alone.

Her aunt had come into the room, fussing once again over what she should wear, repeating how magnificent the house was and extolling the Duke's virtue.

"To-night you will meet the Duke's brother," she said. "You will find him the most charming young man you have ever met in your whole life."

Vina was not listening.

She was tired of hearing her aunt eulogize the Duke and Lord Edgar.

She wished instead that the dinner party could consist of the soldiers and their wives whom her father had entertained.

Better still, a party of Indians with their soft, singsong voices looking, in Vina's opinion, far more attractive than any of the people she had met in England.

When she and her father had travelled about India, and, although the Memsahibs thought it was a mistake to be too familiar with the natives, they had been entertained by Indians of every caste.

Because her father could speak Urdu and several other Indian languages, he was often sent on special missions, quite outside his Regimental duties, to different parts of the country.

After her mother died, Vina had always gone with

him, and they had stayed in small Indian houses as well as in great Palaces.

She had come to be nearly as proficient as her father in Urdu, and he taught her, without her really realising it, how to use her instincts where people were concerned.

'To look beneath the surface and to find,' as he put it with a smile, 'a man or a woman's heart.'

This she had found difficult to do when she first reached England.

Now, however, that she was more accustomed to being with English people, she found herself able to understand them.

Although they were often unaware of it, she would know a great deal more about their personalities than they wished other people to realise.

She was aware that her aunt was frivolous, superficially educated, and tremendously impressed by social position.

It was what Vina had half expected in England.

She was, therefore, fully aware that her aunt was overwhelmed and delighted to be at Quarington and a guest of the Duke.

At the same time, because she had a kind nature and would never knowingly hurt anyone if she could help it, Vina was fond of her.

She could not, however, help thinking that her father would laugh if he knew where she was at the moment and how important it was to his sister-in-law.

He had warned Vina when they were in India not to say too much about their Indian friends when there were English people present.

"All the English are snobs at heart," he said, "and,

what is more, they surround themselves with social barriers to make life even more difficult than it is already."

He had laughed before he added:

"It is something you and I, dearest, will never do! But it is a mistake deliberately to invite criticism by saying so."

"I know what you mean, Papa," Vina had answered, smiling, "and the Major's wife has already given me a lecture about not being too familiar with our Indian servants."

"She would!" Colonel Wallace had laughed. "And she would undoubtedly have a fit if she knew where you and I are going to stay tomorrow night."

They had been the guests of an Indian who had kept a strange shop on the outskirts of Lahore.

In it were pieces of jade and crystal, necklaces which came from Tibet, carvings from the Northern Provinces, and pictures and miniatures of the Rajputs.

Vina was also aware that in another room there were clothes in which a man could disguise himself as a Buddhist monk, or an untouchable.

She had the idea, although she did not ask questions, that these were the things which interested her father.

When they had left he said to her:

"What did you think of our host?"

Vina knew that he really valued her opinions, and she replied slowly:

"He is much cleverer than he wishes to appear. He has a perception that is mystic and which he uses rather than his eyes or his mind. I think, Papa, you find him useful in matters that you wish to keep secret."

Her father had laughed. Then he said:

"Good girl! I will not tell you what the Indian you so

accurately describe said about you, but it was very complimentary!"

Using her intuition now, Vina thought of the Duke.

She wondered what she would feel about him if she did not think of his house, his overwhelming presence, or his handsome face.

"He is not happy," she decided, and knew it was something her aunt Marjory would never believe.

When she was dressed for dinner she thought that the white gown they had chosen in Bond Street was very becoming.

It was draped in the front, and the small bustle at the back was of frills of chiffon which trailed a few metres on the floor behind her.

Her waist was tiny and the bodice above it was embroidered with small turquoises and pearls.

She had known as soon as she saw it that she wanted to possess the gown because the turquoise was a lucky stone in the East.

She had a necklace, given to her by a Maharanee from her own collection, and a bracelet to match it.

They were not large, but the stones were linked together with the exquisite enamelling that the Indians worked so well, and they accentuated the translucence of Vina's skin.

She went downstairs slowly, not thinking that she should wait for her uncle and aunt to collect her.

She entered the Drawing-Room to find there were only two men at the far end of it.

Too late she thought that she should have waited, and she was also earlier than any of the other guests.

The Duke, however, came towards her.

"I must apologize if I am over-punctual, Your

Grace," Vina said, "but I am sure you will understand that living in a soldier's house, I am always afraid of being late."

The Duke laughed.

"And, of course, reprimanded, as I used to be on parade!"

"Uncle Alexander can be very severe." Vina smiled.

They were walking, as they spoke, towards the fireplace, where the other man was still standing. He had not moved when she appeared.

"Let me introduce you to my brother," the Duke said. "Lord Edgar Quary—Miss Vina Wallace!"

Vina put out her hand and, as Lord Edgar took it, she looked up at him and saw an expression in his eyes which startled her.

She did not understand the reason; she only knew that unlike her feelings about the Duke, she thought quite the opposite of his brother.

Because he was worried about Edgar's reaction, the Duke had taken care not to put Vina beside him at dinner.

He was aware that this decision might surprise Lady Wallace.

But, he thought, seeing how attractive Vina was, it would be wise to let Edgar become aware of her attractions before he began to criticise and find fault.

At the same time, he was delighted with Vina and thought his brother was far more fortunate than he had ever expected he might be.

Who could imagine that in the General's family there could be anything so exquisite, so unusual?

She certainly had no resemblance to the girl he had

imagined as Edgar's wife. He was not sure what Edgar had himself expected.

She had seemed graceful and very unusual in her travelling dress and bonnet.

In her evening gown, with her tiny waist encircled by a turquoise satin sash, Vina looked like something out of a picture-book.

The Duke watched her talking quietly, first to the man on one side of her, then to the other.

He thought it would be impossible to imagine that any young girl of her age could be so poised and so unselfconscious.

Yet he noted that Edgar was being somewhat surly to Lady Wallace and undoubtedly drinking far more wine than was good for him.

When the Duke led the men into the Drawing-Room, it was to find the women looking like lovely flowers clustered around the fireplace.

Vina was at the piano, softly playing music he did not recognise.

It was, he thought, the kind of haunting melody which commanded attention although clearly that was not what the pianist intended.

He knew it was a mistake to order Edgar to go and talk to her. He therefore waited until everybody was seated, then walked to the piano.

Vina glanced up at him with a little smile, and went on playing.

"I had no idea you were a musician, Miss Wallace!" the Duke remarked.

"Then you cannot have studied the language when you were in India."

The Duke looked puzzled for a moment, then said:

"You mean that 'Vina' has a special meaning?"

"She is the Goddess of Music."

"So your mother thought when you were born that it was an appropriate name for you!" the Duke said as if to catch her out.

"My mother was very musical," Vina replied, the soft melody still flowing from her fingers. "Therefore, at the time of my birth, my father arranged that a band of Indian musicians who loved her should play in the garden outside the house."

She gave him a mischievous little glance as she went on:

"They played, because they wished to please them, for over twenty-four hours without stopping."

The Duke laughed.

"Then your name is certainly very appropriate, and you must excuse my ignorance."

Vina took her hands from the keyboard.

"Would you rather I stopped?"

"I would like you to do whatever you wish to do," the Duke replied. "I find what you are playing enchanting, although I do not recognise the piece."

"It is not published."

"You mean *you* composed it?"

She nodded, and he said:

"Then I would certainly like you to go on playing. I am sure, Miss Wallace, you express yourself more easily in music than in words."

Vina looked up at him as if she were surprised. Then she said:

"I did not think anyone would understand what I was saying in music, so perhaps it would be wise for me to be careful."

"Are you thinking that what I heard you play would either shock or insult me?" the Duke asked.

Vina laughed.

"Not as bad as that, but people always resent it if you read their thoughts."

"Is that what you have been doing?"

The Duke had no idea why he asked the question.

It suddenly came into his mind, and he was sure he was right; Vina, with her strange beauty, had a perception which he knew was peculiarly prevalent in the East.

As if she knew he was waiting for an answer, Vina said after a moment:

"I try not to read people's secret thoughts . . . but I cannot help knowing what they are really like . . . however hard they pretend to be . . . different."

She spoke quite ingenuously, but to the Duke it was a warning.

As he walked away from the piano, he wondered what Vina would feel about Edgar.

Perhaps, in consequence, all their carefully laid plans would go awry.

chapter three

VINA awoke and, for the first time since she came to Quarington, felt excited.

She had dreamt that she was in India, riding with her father.

When she opened her eyes she remembered that the Duke had said she could ride this morning.

Last night, when she had come to bed, she had asked the maid who looked after her at what time the guests usually rode.

"When it suits 'em, Miss!" the maid had replied. "But none of the ladies gets up early. The gent'men usually go out before breakfast, or immediately afterwards."

Vina looked at the clock beside her bed and saw that it was not yet six o'clock.

That was the time she had always ridden with her father, before the heat of the day, in India, but she

47

thought in England it was unlikely that anyone would be out so early.

In her uncle's house the grooms rarely stirred themselves before seven o'clock.

She thought, therefore, that if she went to the stables, she would not only be able to ride alone, but choose a really spirited horse rather than leave it to the Duke.

Although he had agreed that she could ride what she wished, she was quite certain that because she was so small and unlike Englishwomen who hunted, she would be given a quiet mount.

Her aunt had told her her Lady's-maid would dress her, but because it was something she had always done, she had put on her riding habit herself.

She had no difficulty in putting on her riding boots or fastening the shirt of the expensive habit her aunt had bought for her in London.

She glanced at herself in the mirror as she put on her riding hat with its gauze veil. With a contented little smile she thought that she looked too smart to be a good rider.

It made her more certain than ever that she would be palmed off with a horse that so far as she was concerned, might be a feather bed.

What she wanted was an animal she had to keep under control and which enjoyed the age-old battle between man and beast.

She had no difficulty in finding the stables.

As she had hoped, she discovered the only people in charge were the young stable-lads who had risen before the older grooms.

They touched their forelocks politely as she appeared, and one of them accompanied her as she went from stall to stall, thrilled by the magnificence of the Duke's horses.

She found it difficult to know which one she preferred.

Finally she chose a black stallion that was, she thought, even larger and more outstanding than the rest.

She told the stable-lad to saddle him, but he said:

"That b'aint be no 'orse for a L'dy, Miss."

"That is the one I wish to ride!" Vina replied. "So please saddle him."

The lad looked doubtful, but he did not argue any further.

He had some difficulty, however, in saddling the stallion whose name was Hercules.

Vina helped him by holding the horse and talking to him in the soft, coaxing voice which her father had always used on any difficult animal he had ridden.

At last the stable-lad was able to lead Hercules to the mounting-block.

As Vina climbed into the saddle, she knew it was the most thrilling moment since she had come to England.

She rode out of the stables by the back entrance in case she should encounter anyone coming from the front of the house who might wish to accompany her.

After a few skirmishes, as Hercules tried to show his independence, they were off.

It was not difficult for her to find her way from the paddocks beyond the stable into the flat fields. They were perfect for riding.

There was also a number of low hedges which she took without any difficulty.

Vina then began to explore the countryside with a

feeling in her heart that she had escaped from something rather menacing.

She could not decide what it was except, she told herself, the house was overwhelming and so was her host.

She had the feeling that last night the Duke's guests were looking at her speculatively.

Also that her aunt, for no apparent reason, was watching her in a way she had not done before.

'I suppose Aunt Marjory is afraid I shall do something incorrect and shame her,' she thought with a smile.

She remembered that when she and her father had dined with the Viceroy, her papa had not given a second thought to her behaviour.

Vina had travelled a long way from the house before she told herself she ought to return.

She had a sudden longing not to go back but to go on riding into the far horizon.

Perhaps she would find something more interesting than the dull and uneventful life she had endured for the last year.

She was honest enough to realise that because she was unhappy without her father, any place would at first have seemed dark and uninviting.

It was only with a tremendous effort that she forced herself to behave politely and pleasantly to her uncle and aunt and their friends.

She found that the only way she could forget all she had lost was by reading books.

It was difficult for her to understand that her aunt considered such an occupation a terrible waste of time.

In fact, Lady Wallace was always thinking of ways

of making her put down any book in which she was interested.

This usually meant that she would have to talk to people with whom she had nothing in common or do what her aunt found more amusing than anything else — go shopping.

Now for the moment she was free and, because Hercules was obstreperous to ride, she had first to concentrate on him.

After several tussles, which she won, she felt as if they understood each other.

She was, however, aware that she had to behave correctly, if only for her aunt's sake.

She, therefore, reluctantly turned Hercules's head towards home.

As she did so she was aware that somewhere in the distance there was a lone rider.

She thought perhaps it was one of the Duke's guests, and the last thing she wished to do at the moment was to have a banal conversation about the weather.

Worse still, she might have to listen to some Englishman paying her fatuous compliments.

There were several men in the party who, she had realised last night, had looked at her with a glint of admiration in their eye.

She was quite sure, she thought scornfully, that they had no brains.

Their conversation would be entirely about racing or the hunts in which they had taken part during the winter.

It was what the men, young and old, talked about round her uncle's dining-room table. She wished she could have discussed the Regimental events in which he could no longer take part.

Everything in India had been so different.

She had listened while the senior officers had talked to her father of the Russian infiltration amongst the tribesmen on the North-West Frontier, the terrors of Thuggee, of the horror of *Suttee*.

Apart from that, there had been her father's mysterious visits.

They were very secret, but, on his return, officers as concerned as he was with the hidden undercurrents of insurrection would come to talk to him about what he had discovered.

Although it was reprehensible, Vina would eavesdrop.

However, when after the first time she admitted to her father what she had done, he had only laughed.

"You are intelligent enough, my poppet," he said, "to realise that you hold my life in your hand. One unwary word could mean my death, if nobody else's."

"You know I will be discreet, Papa, and never do anything that could possibly hurt you. At the same time, although I am frightened by what you do, I find it very thrilling!"

Her father had kissed her, but he had not forbidden her to eavesdrop.

She, therefore, learned many secrets which would have horrified the "powers that be," had they been aware of her knowledge of them.

But because he trusted her, her father often made use of her intuition.

"What did you think of the man who came to see me yesterday?" he would ask.

He knew she had overheard what had been said, though the visitor had not been aware of it.

Sometimes Vina would reply:

"He is honest and trustworthy, but rather stupid."

"That is what I thought myself," her father would say.

Or else her reply might be:

"He is interested only in money. If somebody offered him more than you pay him, he would not hesitate to accept it."

"How can you be aware of that?" Colonel Wallace had enquired.

"When he told you what he had spent in obtaining the information you wanted," Vina answered, "he was asking more than he had actually expended, also his voice was greedy."

Her father had put his arm around his daughter's shoulders.

"I should not allow you to do this," he had said, "but you are a great help to me."

"How can all those days be over?" Vina had asked herself despairingly after she had come to England.

Sometimes, when the conversation was so commonplace, she had found it hard to even make a pretence of listening to what was being said.

Now, because she wanted to escape the horse rider who might or might not be looking for her, she put Hercules at a high hedge.

It was different from those she had jumped before; but she cleared it without difficulty.

Then at the end of the field she saw yet another hedge.

To her delight, Hercules seemed to fly over them.

Vina saw a flat piece of land in front of her, and she

53

thought she had certainly evaded her pursuer, if that was what he was.

Hercules settled down to a trot and Vina thought of her father.

It was therefore a shock when a voice behind her asked sharply:

"How can you take those jumps in such an irresponsible manner on a horse you have no right to be riding?"

As he spoke, the Duke came alongside her and, as Vina turned her face to look at him, she realised he was angry.

She had no idea how concerned he had been when he arrived at the stables about ten minutes after she had left.

He had asked for Hercules to be saddled only to be told that the horse was already being ridden by one of his guests.

The Head Groom had come hurrying towards the Duke as he started to interrogate the stable-boy.

"We didn't expect ye so early, Y'Grace..." he began, but the Duke interrupted him.

"I have just learned that Hercules is being ridden, without my permission," he said sharply.

The Head Groom looked at the empty stall as if he could not believe his eyes. Then he said angrily to the stable-boy:

"What d'you mean by lettin' someone take 'Is Grace's 'orse?"

"'Er insisted on havin' im!" the lad said defiantly.

"*Her?*" the Duke exclaimed. "Are you telling me that a *Lady* is riding Hercules?"

"Aye, Y'Grace."

"Saddle Wellington!" the Duke peremptorily commanded.

Three minutes later he left the stable by the back entrance, the stable lad telling him the direction Vina had taken.

He had no idea where she could have gone except that the surrounding fields were flat and an invitation to any rider.

He thought apprehensively that if Hercules was up to his usual tricks, she might be lying at the bottom of a fence or be unconscious in a ditch.

He had quite expected to encounter Hercules riderless, making his own way back to the stable.

It was with a deep sense of relief, therefore, that the Duke finally saw far in the distance the horse and rider he was seeking.

It was then he realised that Vina was running away from him.

He first of all thought it an impertinence; then, as she took fences he would himself have found difficult, if not impossible, he felt his temper rising.

He had bought Hercules from a friend who said quite frankly that he had found the stallion too hard to handle, and quite dangerous.

"You are the only man who would, I think, be able to control him," he had told the Duke.

The Duke had discovered he was right, and it was a challenge he enjoyed.

Although the stallion was now far less obstreperous, he had not yet allowed anyone else to ride him.

With horror he watched Vina taking one fence after another, expecting at any moment to see her fall to the ground.

If she did not break her neck, he thought, she would certainly be severely injured in one way or another.

Now, as he saw the ease with which she was riding, he could hardly believe he was not dreaming.

"I . . . I am sorry, Your Grace," she said in a quiet voice, "if I have done anything wrong, but you did say I could have a horse that was spirited."

"Spirited!" the Duke exclaimed.

Suddenly he laughed.

"I do not believe it!" he said. "How can you ride a horse which I myself have difficulty in holding?"

Vina smiled and bent forward to pat Hercules on the neck.

"He is magnificent!" she said. "And I think perhaps we understand each other."

"Are you telling me that you have some magic power over horses, as if you were a Lion-Tamer?" the Duke asked.

Vina shook her head.

"I do not think it is magic," she replied, "but Papa said if you gave animals love, real love, which they understand, then they respond in a different way to people who, although they may not be aware of it, are really frightened of them."

She was thinking as she spoke of the elephants in India who loved their Mahouts and the tiger cub which her father had kept as a pet after its mother had been shot.

It had been as adorable as any kitten.

Vina had cried when eventually her father had been forced, because they were moving to another part of India, to send it to a Zoo.

She had lain awake for nights worrying that the cub

would miss them, and feel lonely and neglected.

They rode for a few minutes in silence. Then the Duke said:

"I have to concede, Miss Wallace, that you are, without exception, the best rider I have ever met, but you have also nearly caused my heart to stop beating."

Vina looked surprised for a moment. Then she said:

"You thought Hercules would throw me?"

"I was sure he would do so," the Duke replied, "and I had visions of you being seriously injured."

"I . . . I suppose," Vina said hesitatingly, "that I should . . . apologise for taking him . . . without asking you . . . but . . . to be honest . . . I thought no one would be up so early . . . and that I would be back in the stables before anybody had time to worry about me."

"I was early too," the Duke admitted, "because I did not sleep well."

This was true because he had been concerned about Edgar; at the same time, he had wondered if there would be any real alternative to his marrying Vina Wallace.

He knew now that he had seen her that she was not at all the sort of wife Edgar would appreciate, nor would she be likely to reform him.

He was well aware that Edgar's women—and there had been a great number of them—were noisy and tawdry.

In fact, in his opinion, they were of a coarse type who were at their best at riotous parties at which too much wine was served.

Now that he had seen Vina, the duke could not imagine Edgar finding her in any way to his taste.

His choices were invariably flamboyant, overdressed and over-bejewelled. Their conversation was certainly not suitable for anybody as young as Vina.

Then, as he had still been awake when the dawn was breaking, he had told himself that he was being very stupid.

Perhaps with the General behind her, Vina would be able to curb some of Edgar's wild extravagances and at least have the whip hand, because she held the purse-strings.

As dawn broke, the Duke was still sleepless. It was then that he had decided to go riding.

Now, as their horses moved together over the flat field in the direction of the house, Vina said again:

"I am sorry . . . I have behaved badly . . . but still it has been the most exciting and wonderful thing that has happened to me since I . . . came to England."

"Do you miss India very much?"

"To me it is like being shut out of Paradise."

"Are you saying that you do not like this country?"

"To be honest . . . I find it very . . . dull."

He looked at her in astonishment and she said quickly:

"But please . . . do not repeat that to my uncle and aunt. It has been very kind of them to have me . . . but they do not understand how different it was being with . . . Papa."

"I should have thought you would have found the Regimental quarters in India rather constricting," the Duke remarked. "I have always understood that the *Memsahibs* lived a somewhat monotonous life."

Vina laughed.

"My life with Papa was certainly not monotonous! We travelled all over the country, and I think perhaps you would be shocked at some of the strange places in which we have stayed, and the people we have known."

Suddenly the Duke was aware why Vina's father had been spoken of with so much respect.

He remembered, as he had forgotten before, that the Secretary of State for India had said to him one evening in London:

"I hear you have Sir Alexander Wallace as a neighbour in the country."

The Duke agreed, and he went on:

"His brother David is one of the most brilliant men we have ever had in India."

The Duke had looked surprised; then somebody had come to interrupt them and he had not thought of it again.

Now he had an idea of the work in which Vina's father had been engaged and he understood what she was feeling.

They rode in single file through a ride in the wood, and then were in the Park with the great house standing just ahead of them.

The Duke looked at it with satisfaction before he said:

"I want you to like and admire Quarington."

"It is . . . very impressive."

The Duke waited to hear the eulogies which usually came from anyone who looked at or talked about the house.

Then, as Vina did not speak, he said almost as if he forced her to be more appreciative:

"You see the tower at the far end? It is all that remains of the Norman Castle which was built on this site after William of Normandy won the Battle of Hastings."

Vina looked and saw that the tower altered the otherwise perfect symmetry of the house which she guessed rightly was of the Georgian period.

"It is known," the Duke went on as if he wished to command her attention, "as the 'Tower of Despair!'"

"What an unhappy name!" Vina exclaimed. "But, why?"

"The Norman Baron who built Quarington took a large number of prisoners who had ferociously fought against him."

The Duke looked at Vina to see if she was interested, and went on:

"He then informed them that he had no intention of allowing them to escape, and because they had killed so many of his men, they would remain his prisoners for life!"

"Incarcerated in the Tower?"

"Yes, but he was merciful enough to allow them, when they wished, to go up onto the roof."

The way the Duke spoke told Vina that this was not the end of the story, and she looked at him enquiringly.

"There was, of course, a moat all around the Castle in those days, but now only a very small part of it is left beneath the Tower."

"You mean the prisoners ... threw themselves into it!" Vina said, understanding where the story was leading.

"Exactly!" the Duke answered. "The family history says that no less than a hundred men perished in that way."

Vina shuddered.

"I think if I owned your house I would want to sweep away the fear they must have felt before they drowned."

Since this was the first time the suggestion had been made to him, the Duke looked at her in surprise.

"I think it would be sacrilege," he said, "to destroy anything that has been preserved for so many generations. The house has been built and rebuilt, but the Tower of Despair has always remained."

"Then I can only hope that there will be no more prisoners in it," Vina said, "and if there are, that I am not one of them!"

She spoke lightly, but there was a frown between the Duke's eyes as she quickened Hercules's pace, and he followed her.

*   *   *

Back at the house Vina changed out of her riding clothes, then went down to the Breakfast Room.

As she half expected, there were only the younger members of the house-party because the more elderly ladies like her aunt had breakfast in their bedrooms or the *Boudoirs* which adjoined them.

There was no sign of the Duke, and she thought he must have eaten very quickly or else was taking longer than she had in changing.

She did not tell anyone he had been riding.

For the first time it crossed her mind that it was a rather reprehensible thing to have done without a chaperon.

It was only when she had come to England that she had realised how many restrictions existed for a young girl.

She supposed had she spent much time at Hill Stations or in Calcutta or Bombay that she would have found the same in India.

But she and her father, especially after her mother had died, had always been on the move.

She had forgotten, therefore, that it was incorrect for a woman to ride without being accompanied by a groom, and perhaps even more improper to ride alone with a young man.

The Duke, she thought, certainly did not come into that category.

At the same time, she had noticed vaguely on the previous night that a beautiful member of the Party, Lady Halford, had been very possessive towards him.

She might be annoyed if she thought he had been spending any time with her.

"What are you going to do this morning, Miss Wallace?" one of the men in the party asked.

"I have not yet seen my aunt to ask her what she wishes to do," Vina replied.

"What I would like to do," the man said, "is to take you driving. I am sure you would enjoy seeing our host's estate—a model of its kind."

"Now, Edmund, you are rushing your fences as usual!" one of the others intervened. "I was going to ask Miss Wallace if she would like me to show her the hothouses. They are some of the best in the country."

"I have a better idea," another man chimed in. "I will take Miss Wallace riding."

They all looked at Vina as he spoke, but when she had finished her breakfast, she rose from the table.

"It is very kind of you," she said, "but first I have to consult my aunt and, secondly, I want above everything else to see the Library."

She walked away as she spoke, not realising that all three gentlemen were staring after her in astonishment.

Later, Vina went with Lady Wallace and several other ladies to see the hothouses.

When they returned, the Butler showed her to the Library.

It was as fine as she had hoped, books reaching from floor to ceiling, with a balcony all along one wall.

Vina longed to be able to spend the rest of the day there, uninterrupted.

After luncheon several of the party wished to go riding, and the Duke said he would take them to see the racecourse he was having laid out on the other side of the Park.

There was no question this time of Vina riding Hercules.

While the horse she was given was, as the Duke had promised, spirited, it could not compare in any way with the great stallion.

As if the Duke were well aware of what she was thinking, his eyes twinkled as he said quietly to her so that nobody else could hear:

"I was afraid you would be disappointed."

"I was too polite to say so," Vina replied. "But at the same time, there is no comparison."

"I quite agree with you," the Duke said. "But I thought that Hercules has had enough excitement for one day."

She laughed; he thought it was a very young, spontaneous, and very pretty sound.

Then they were all riding towards the new racecourse, though Lord Edgar was not in the party.

Vina did not miss him; but the Duke did and there had been a harshness in his voice as he asked the Butler:

"Is Lord Edgar not coming with us?"

"No, Your Grace, His Lordship is playing Billiards."

The Duke did not say anything, but he wondered, as he rode after the rest of the party, what Edgar was up to.

He had always been unpredictable, and it seemed extraordinary that if he had made up his mind to propose to Vina Wallace he was making no effort at all to make her acquaintance.

Lady Wallace thought the same thing.

After tea, when there was still no sign of Lord Edgar, and she was just about to suggest to Vina that she rest before dinner, she realised she had disappeared.

"Where has my niece gone?" she asked the man who was just finishing his cup of tea.

"She said something about going to the Library," he replied.

"Books!" Lady Wallace sniffed disparagingly. "That girls thinks about nothing but reading! As I told her, she will be blind before she is fifty!"

She looked up expectantly as the door opened, and Lord Edgar came into the room.

One of the gentlemen looked up at him to say:

"Hello, Edgar! Where have you been? I missed you this afternoon."

"I have been drinking," Lord Edgar said in a somewhat slurred and uncompromising voice.

Then as he saw Lady Wallace he walked towards her.

"Where is your niece?" he enquired.

"She is in the Library," Lady Wallace replied, simpering a little as she spoke.

Without another word Lord Edgar turned on his heel and left the room.

Lady Wallace gave a sigh of relief and, without realising it, clasped her hands together.

This was the moment for which she had waited. This is what she had planned; now her dreams had come true.

*   *   *

In the Library, Vina collected half-a-dozen books, finding each one more irresistible than the last.

As she carried them from the shelves to the window-seat of rich red velvet, she thought that never had she seen so many books she wanted to read.

She wondered wistfully if she would ever have time to devour even a few before they went home.

The difficulty was to know where to begin.

She turned over the pages of two of those she had selected before finally she opened a third, being immediately absorbed by the very first paragraph she read.

As usual, she was swept away into another world and did not hear the Library door open or be aware that there was anybody but herself in the room.

Then Lord Edgar was standing beside her, and she looked up at him.

Her immediate thought was that it was infuriating to be interrupted, and she hoped he would not want to stay and talk to her.

Then, she thought, there was a strange expression on his face before he said in a voice that was unexpectedly harsh:

"As we both know why you are here, I suggest that the sooner I say what has to be said, the better."

Because of the way he spoke and what she thought was almost an aggressive look in his eyes, Vina was surprised.

"What it amounts to," Lord Edgar went on, "is that

the sooner we are married, the better it will be as far as I am concerned. What date do you suggest?"

Now, as Vina stared at him in bewilderment, it flashed through her mind that he must have had too much to drink.

"I . . . I do not understand . . ." she began.

"Of course you understand!" Lord Edgar said sharply. "And it is ridiculous to think it should be tied up in ribbons when it is quite simply a commercial bargain."

He seemed almost to spit the words out.

"A . . . A bargain?" she faltered.

"Whatever you like to call it, that is what it is," he said. "You want my title. I want your money. We should deal quite well together."

Now he was sneering, and Vina rose slowly to her feet.

"I am afraid . . . My Lord," she said, "I do not know . . . what you are . . . talking . . . about."

"Come on!" he said. "Do not play the simpleton with me. Your uncle and aunt have the whole thing tied up with my brother, and, as I have said, all I want to know is the date. There are quite a number of people interested in that!"

Vina took a step in the direction of the door and, as if he realised she was trying to leave the room, Lord Edgar said:

"It cannot be very difficult for you to make up your mind whether it be two weeks', three weeks', or four weeks' time. I have told you, as far as I am concerned, the quicker the better."

Now Vina looked at him a little nervously and once again went towards the door.

Angrily Lord Edgar stepped in front of her.

"Are you playing hard to get?" he asked. "Or are you just rebuking me for not going down on one knee and kissing your hand? If that is what you want, and I cannot get a word out of you in any other way, why, dammit, I will do it!"

"I honestly . . . do not know . . . what you are talking . . . about," Vina protested.

"Then let me put it in plain English," Lord Edgar answered. "I want to know the date of our wedding because I am asking you to marry me!"

Vina stiffened; then she said very quietly:

"My answer, Lord Edgar, is no! I have no intention of marrying you, but . . . I am sure it is an honour that . . . you should . . . ask me."

She could not help a sarcastic note creeping into her voice, even though it trembled a little because she was frightened.

She was quite certain that Lord Edgar was drunk and did not know what he was saying.

Even so, she had never been spoken to in such a way by any man, and she thought it insulting.

Once again she would have moved towards the door, but Lord Edgar was there before her.

"You cannot mean you are getting to 'cry off' at the last moment? The whole thing is arranged by my brother and your uncle and aunt, and it is no use either of us kicking against the pricks."

"W-what . . . are you s-saying?" Vina asked.

Lord Edgar stared at her.

"Do you honestly tell me they have said nothing to you?"

"About my being . . . married? No . . . of course . . . not!"

He looked at her as if he still did not believe she was telling the truth, then he said:

"It seems extraordinary to me, but it does not matter. Now that you know what is going to happen, you will just have to put up with it, as I have."

"Put up with . . . what?"

"Our being married," he said, as if she was half-witted.

"But . . . I have no intention of . . . marrying you . . . nor . . . anyone whom I do not . . . love!"

"Oh, God, is that what is worrying you? I would love anyone who would pay my debts and let me live the life I enjoy."

Vina looked over his shoulder at the door.

She could not reach it unless she pushed past him, and she had the frightening feeling he might touch her and prevent her from leaving.

She drew in her breath before she said:

"If . . . as you . . . say . . . my uncle and aunt have really connived with your . . . brother for us to be . . . married . . . surely . . . it is something which . . . concerns us . . . not them? And while I am very honoured, Lord Edgar, by your . . . proposal, my . . . answer is no!"

It was an effort to say the words, and they came to her in a hesitating, frightened manner because she was trembling.

Lord Edgar took a step towards her.

"Now, listen," he said, "this is something which you cannot back out of. Your uncle is your legal Guardian, and by the law you have to obey him."

He paused before he went on:

"I may make you a rotten husband, but I will try to be polite in public. Anyway, we will have enough money for you to live the sort of life you want; and I can live mine."

He moved a little closer to her as he said:

"After all, it may not be as bad as you think."

Then, with a swiftness of movement which took him by surprise, Vina reached the door.

She pulled it open, and before Lord Edgar could stop her, she ran away down the passage with the speed of a frightened deer.

For a moment he considered going after her, and then realised she would by now have reached the hall, where there were footmen on duty.

He took a handkerchief out of his pocket and mopped his forehead.

"Curse the little fool!" he swore angrily.

chapter four

VINA ran upstairs to her bedroom.

There was nobody there, as her maid had not yet come to arrange her bath; for a moment she looked around her wildly.

Then it occurred to her that her aunt might come in to talk to her, so she locked the door.

She could hardly believe that what Lord Edgar said was true.

Yet she was intelligent enough to realise that it was not only a possibility but it explained what she had sensed in her uncle's and aunt's attitudes before they arrived in Quarington.

This was why her aunt had kept stressing what an attractive young man Lord Edgar was.

It was also definitely part of her excitement at being a guest of the Duke.

Vina seated herself on the chaise longue which stood

at the bottom of the bed and tried to think clearly what had happened and what she could do about it.

She was still trembling because of the way in which Lord Edgar had spoken to her.

Yet her horror at what he had suggested was far deeper than the emotions he had aroused with his rudeness or the shock of what he had told her.

She knew that ever since, she had thought him repulsive, and, as her intuition had never failed her, she was sure she was not mistaken.

"How could I marry a man like . . . that?" she asked herself. "Somebody who . . . wants me only for . . . my money?"

When she had first been told of the enormous fortune left to her father, she had simply been glad that all the kind acts he had done for other people had been recognised.

Then, when she understood that as he was no longer alive the money was hers, she had wanted to help the people of India.

She had, therefore, instructed her uncle's Solicitor, who had taken charge of her affairs, to send money to a number of people who had worked for her father.

These included the servants who had shown him mounting devotion during his lifetime.

What she had suggested had not come to an enormous sum, but her aunt nevertheless had told her to think of herself before she started "throwing her money around like water."

Vina had not replied, but had felt an overwhelming need for her father's advice on how she could expend her fortune for the good of other people.

When she was a child she could remember her mother saying to her father:

"I hope you do not mind, darling, but I gave fifty *rupees* to our tailor's wife. She is expecting their eighth child."

"I should think it impossible for him to afford so many!" her father had remarked.

"That is true and he has got into debt," Mrs. Wallace had answered. "At the same time, he is such a nice little man, and although we cannot afford it, I felt I had to help them."

"Of course you did," her husband answered, and put his arms around her. "At the same time, if I did not control your kind heart, we should be bankrupt!"

He had been teasing her mother, but Vina had known there was a grain of truth in what he said.

Her mother could not bear to see anybody suffering for lack of food—all too prevalent in India.

When she was older, Vina realised that her mother had often economised by not having a new gown so that she could help those who were hungry or ill.

She was aware that if her aunt had anything to do with it, all her money would be spent on clothes and fripperies.

While Vina wanted to buy books for herself, she was not particularly interested in what she wore.

She had been thinking, during the last month, when she learnt that the money had been paid into her uncle's Bank and the jewels had arrived at their house, what she would do in the future.

She thought that the best thing to do would be to talk it over quietly with her uncle.

Unfortunately, the opportunity had not arrived before

73

she was told they were to stay at Quarington.

After that, her aunt had left her no time to think of anything except clothes.

Now, as she thought it over, she understood what had been planned.

The whole idea was so horrifying that her first impulse was to leave the house immediately, never to see Lord Edgar again.

Then, because her father had taught her to reason things out logically, she remembered how Lord Edgar had said that her uncle was her Guardian and that she had to do what he told her.

She knew this was true.

It was not really surprising, considering that in India all marriages were arranged by the parents of the bride and bridegroom.

The majority of Hindu girls never saw their bridegrooms until the wedding ceremony took place.

Vina, however, had a horror of arranged marriages ever since one of the young wives of an important Maharajah whom her father was visiting had confided in her.

She was a young girl of fifteen who had been married for only two months, and Vina, visiting the women's quarters in the Palace, had found her sobbing bitterly.

She had wandered away to explore part of the Palace alone, and as she was so upset by the girl's unhappiness, she had sat down and tried to comfort her.

Vina could speak Urdu quite fluently, and she soon learned why the girl was so unhappy.

First of all, she was lonely, and as the latest and youngest of the Maharajah's wives, the others were bullying her.

Then, as Vina knew already, the Maharajah was a very old man and in ill health.

"It is a great honour for my father that I should be his wife," the young woman sobbed, "but the Astrologers say he will soon die, and then I must die too!"

"You do . . . not mean . . . ?" Vina exclaimed in horror.

"Although the British have forbidden it," the girl answered, "the other wives will all commit *suttee* on our Lord's funeral pyre."

Vina had not known what to say.

She was well aware that the British, after they had conquered India, had done everything in their power to stamp out *suttee*.

But it was a tradition for the widows to throw themselves onto the burning flames which consumed their husband's body.

It had been a custom in India for centuries, and it was very difficult to prevent an action which was considered sacred.

Vina had spoken to her father about it and he had agreed that *suttee* was barbaric and cruel.

At the same time, it took place.

The Maharajahs, who had the power of life and death in their own Provinces, considered it right and proper that their wives should die with them.

"But Ajsha is only fifteen, Papa!" Vina had expostulated.

"I know, my dearest, and I realise how much it upsets you," her father had said. "I will do everything in my power to prevent it from taking place when the Maharajah dies, but I doubt if I will be successful."

A month later Vina learned that the Maharajah was

dead, and although the British had tried to prevent it, his wives had all committed *suttee*.

It had made Vina feel more strongly than ever that arranged marriages were cruel, however advantageous they might be to the parents.

She saw that for the bride it could be terrifying, not only from the point of view of *suttee,* but how could a girl of fifteen be expected to love an old man who was practically on his deathbed?

Remembering Ajsha made Vina think how frightening it would be to be confronted for the first time by a man to whom one had taken an instant dislike.

She herself had known what she wanted, and that was to be as happy as her father and mother had been.

Wherever they went, whatever they were doing, however uncomfortable it was, nothing was more important than that they were together.

She would have been very obtuse if she had not realised that when her father was away on one of his mysterious trips, her mother was worried and anxious.

When he returned, usually unexpectedly and unannounced, her mother's cry of joy and the eager way in which she ran to her husband's arms seemed to light the room.

It was as if it came from some Divine Power.

"Oh, darling, you are back!" her mother would exclaim.

Her voice was like a paean of happiness that seemed to vibrate in the atmosphere.

"That is how I want to feel when I am married," Vina told herself.

She knew now that never in a thousand years could

she feel anything but horror at being married to Lord Edgar.

Because her father had taught her how to look into the heart of a man, she realised that he was everything she disliked and, what was more, he frightened her.

She had felt herself flinch when men tried to sit too near to her or hold her hand for longer than was necessary, and, when she was no longer a child, to kiss her.

She had learnt to avoid such intimacy with an adroitness that was part of her intelligence.

If somebody was inclined to be familiar, she either disappeared before they were in the house or managed never to be alone with them.

It was instinctive but very sensible and prevented her from being involved in any unpleasant arguments.

Now she was faced with something far more difficult and very much more frightening.

Trying to think objectively, she realised that if she told her aunt that Lord Edgar had mentioned marriage, Lady Wallace would be delighted.

Vina was certain now that it had been her idea that she should marry Lord Edgar.

She was well aware that living in the vicinity of Quarington and never being invited by the Duke to a party had irked her aunt.

Lady Wallace had longed to know and be on intimate terms with all the most important people in the County.

There was no one more important than the Duke; yet she and the General had never dined at Quarington and Vina could remember her frequently complaining about it.

Slowly everything fell into place like a jigsaw puzzle.

Vina realised that every pressure would be brought to bear on her to accept Lord Edgar's extraordinary proposal.

"How can this happen to me?" she asked. "And how could Papa have guessed, when he saved the Maharajah's life, that he would leave him so much money?"

She had been slightly apprehensive when she had first learnt what a huge sum it was.

Now she knew that as far as she was concerned, it was a tragedy.

"If it is not Lord Edgar, then perhaps Aunt Marjory will find somebody just as important . . . and just as unpleasant!"

She felt herself tremble at the thought of being touched by such a man, and perhaps being forced to bear his children.

The idea made Vina jump to her feet and walk to the window as if she suddenly needed air.

Although she was only vaguely aware of what happened between a man and a woman when they made love, she could not have lived in India without realising that childbirth could be a very painful process.

Women in India conceived one child after another, until, at an early age, they were physically exhausted.

Vina thought apprehensively that if she were married to Lord Edgar, he would want her to stay in the country and have children while he went to London to enjoy himself.

Looking back, she could remember a great many things that had been said about him which had meant nothing to her at the time.

Yet they had somehow remained in her mind.

Lady Farringham, her aunt's greatest friend, was an

inveterate gossip and never came to the house without mulling over titbits of scandal concerning their neighbours.

Vina had heard Lord Edgar spoken of again and again.

She had not been in the least interested, except that she realised that everything Lady Farringham related meant something special to her aunt.

She could also remember hearing her aunt say:

"No wonder I hear the Duke has been remonstrating with his brother for behaving in such an outrageous way."

This was after Lady Farringham had described a midnight Steeple-chase in which two riders had been badly injured and three horses had to be destroyed.

Vina, who was invariably thinking of something else when Lady Farringham was there, had been alerted because of the horses.

She thought that any man who could destroy an animal in such a way ought to be put in prison.

She had even spoken about it to her uncle.

"Surely," she had said to the General, "somebody should stop these Steeple-chases at night when horses are forced over jumps which are too high for them? The riders are obviously incapable of controlling them!"

"Silly young fools, too drunk to know what they are doing," the General had replied.

"Supposing you spoke to them, Uncle Alexander? Would they not listen to you?"

"In any Regiment under my command I would make sure they did!" he had replied. "But it is the Duke of Quarington's job to see that his brother behaves himself."

There was no more to be said, but Vina had grieved over the horses and had talked it over with her uncle's groom.

"'Tis a real shame, Miss Vina—that's wot it is!" he said. "I wouldn't let any of the 'orses here take part in any of 'Is Lordship's Chases—that I wouldn't!"

Vina had thought that as her uncle's horses were over-weight and under-exercised, it was unlikely they would take part in any sort of race.

She was, however, too tactful to say so, only thankful that for whatever reason, they were not in any danger.

Now all this and a great many other things that had been said about Lord Edgar came into her mind.

She was still thinking desperately of what she should do, when the maid who was looking after her knocked on the door.

Automatically, because she was trying to think, Vina bathed and put on the first gown that the maid brought from the wardrobe.

Her hair was arranged, and it was only when she was sitting in front of the mirror that the maid said:

"I think, Miss, this gown wants something round the neck. Shall I bring you your jewel-box?"

With an effort Vina forced herself to understand that she had been asked a question.

"My . . . jewel-box?" she repeated vaguely.

It was then she remembered that her aunt had insisted that she bring with her to Quarington the fantastic jewels her father had been left in the Maharajah's will.

She had been surprised because she had thought herself that although they were a very impressive collection, they were far too large and too spectacular to be worn by anyone as young as herself.

She would have liked to suggest to her aunt that they should be left behind.

Then it struck her that perhaps her possessions would be discussed amongst the guests at Quarington, and her aunt would want to show them off because they were Indian.

Now, as if they were something unpleasant, Vina said quickly:

"No, no! Of course not! I have no wish to wear any jewels!"

The maid looked surprised because of the forceful way in which she had spoken.

Then, because Vina knew she was correct in saying her neck looked bare, she arranged a thin band of velvet ribbon around it.

Taking a small orchid from the vase which stood on her dressing-table, she attached it to the ribbon.

"That looks ever so nice, Miss!" the maid said admiringly. "I've never seen anyone wear a flower like that before!"

"It is quite comfortable," Vina said as she smiled, "and I am content to leave the necklaces and tiaras to the ladies who are married."

The maid giggled. Then she said:

"An' that's wot you'll be soon, Miss!"

There was a knowing look in her eye which told Vina that the servants must be aware of why she had come to stay, and of Lord Edgar's intentions.

She was not surprised.

Servants the world over always knew what was going on around them.

At the same time, she felt as if prison bars were closing around her and there was no escape.

It was then, as she rose to go downstairs, she began to pray frantically, desperately, that someone would save her.

*　　*　　*

The Duke, returning quietly in the early hours of the morning from Lady Halford's bedroom, yawned.

Surprisingly, it was not only because he had not slept well the previous night, or the fact that the lovemaking in which he had just been taking part had been fiery and exhausting.

It was, although he was not prepared to admit it to himself, because he had not been concentrating as wholeheartedly as he should have done on Irene Halford.

She was certainly everything a man could desire: beautiful, witty, exotic, and, as far as he was concerned, in love with him.

The Duke was aware that, previously, he had not only enjoyed the hours they had been together, but also had found it impossible to think of anything else.

Yet, tonight, stirred physically as he was by Irene's expertise, he kept seeing the stricken look in Vina's eyes, and knew that something was very wrong.

Edgar had been drinking heavily, which was nothing unusual.

But he did not look like a man who had achieved his objective and, glancing from one to the other, the Duke was apprehensive.

He could hardly believe that Vina, despite the fact that she was different from what he had expected, would have turned down his brother's proposal of marriage.

In fact, he was certain she would not be allowed to do so.

If Lady Wallace had made up her mind that she was to be affiliated with the Quary family, Vina, as the ward of the General, would not be able to refuse what had been arranged for her.

When Vina had come to the Drawing-Room, where they had assembled before dinner, the Duke had been aware that she was very pale, and that her whole body was tense.

He had not had a chance to speak to her.

Then at the dining-table he could see her eyes, and he thought there was an expression of shock in them that was unmistakable.

He decided he would speak to her after dinner, but, when the gentlemen joined the ladies in the Drawing-Room, there was no sign of Vina.

He thought it would be tactless to ask where she had gone.

There was also no chance to speak to his brother, who went off to the Billiard Room with another man.

When Edgar appeared, just as the Duke was going to bed, he was staggering unsteadily.

Irene Halford had not come to Quarington without making it very clear to the Duke what she expected, and what she intended to have.

Without insulting her, it would have been quite impossible for him not to go to her bedroom, where she was waiting.

As he, too, was very experienced in the art of making love, there was no question of his not making her happy.

It was what he had anticipated when he asked her to stay.

Yet some part of his mind remained detached and was concerned with the problem of Vina Wallace and his brother.

"Surely you do not intend to leave me?" Irene asked when he said he would return to his own room.

"To be honest, I am tired," the Duke admitted. "I did not sleep last night and I think, too, I should leave you to rest."

"I can rest when you are not there," she protested.

Somehow he had managed to extricate himself from her arms.

As he shut her door softly behind him and started to walk down the corridor, he no longer thought about her.

It was then he saw at the very end of the long corridor, which was the whole length of the centre block of the building, there was someone else.

The Duke stopped dead, having no wish to be seen.

He was then aware that a figure looking almost like a ghost in the dim light was going away from him.

He wondered who it could possibly be.

Only his most important guests slept in this part of the building containing the Ducal Suite, which he occupied himself.

Then he saw the figure ahead go right to the very end of the corridor, pass a secondary staircase which led to the other floors, and turn right.

This led into another passage, which led to the oldest part of the house.

It was so surprising a thing for any guest to do at this

time of the night that the Duke was curious.

He had put Irene on this floor for obvious reasons, but the majority of guests were in the East Wing.

Then he remembered there were three exceptions: the General and Lady Wallace, who he thought in the circumstances were entitled to the best of the State Rooms and, beside them, their niece, Vina.

His instinct told him it was Vina he had just seen disappearing into the passage which led to the Tower of Despair.

It was then that his whole mind was suddenly alert with what that might portend.

The Duke, because he was in many ways unusual and different from his contemporaries, had a vivid imagination.

He remembered exactly what he had said to Vina when he had told her about the Tower of Despair, and he connected it with the stricken look he had seen in her eyes and the pallor of her face.

Suddenly he knew it was a warning he could not ignore.

Quickening his pace, he passed the door of his own Suite, reached the end of the corridor and turned, as the ghost-like figure had done, into the passage which connected the Tower with the main building.

It was narrow and unlit except for the moonlight coming through the long windows which the Architect had thought appropriate to match the Tower itself.

After that, as the Duke knew only too well, there were only arrow-slits.

And yet, when he reached the Tower, half-way up there was enough moonlight for him to find his way to the narrow, twisting, stone steps.

These descended to the main entrance, which was on the ground floor; below that were the dungeons in which the prisoners had been held.

There was no sign of Vina, and he thought, as he moved slowly and soundlessly in his bedroom slippers over the worn steps, that he had been mistaken.

She must have turned down the secondary staircase, although why she should do so in the middle of the night he had no idea.

Then, as he reached the top of the Tower, he was aware that the door was open and the moonlight was pouring in.

He knew then that he had not been mistaken and, as he pushed the door farther open and bent his head, he saw that his supposition had been correct.

Vina was standing by the crenellated battlements, looking down into what remained of the moat.

It was the Duke's father who had had the sides of the moat made strong enough to prevent any water from escaping and who had cleaned out the spring which fed it.

The stagnant water was piped away when it became overfull, into the fields not far away from the house.

The Duke was aware that what remained of the moat was very deep.

If anyone was so foolish as to fall from the top of the Tower, they would doubtless be concussed and drown before they could be rescued.

He slipped out onto the roof, and once he was out in the open air he straightened himself.

By the light which came from the moon and the stars he could see that Vina was wearing only a soft, diaphanous *négligée* and that her hair was flowing over her shoulders.

With one hand she was holding on to the crenellated battlement.

She looked so fragile and ethereal that the Duke felt she had only to take one step forward and she would disappear from view.

Slowly he moved towards her, saying as he did so in a conversational tone:

"I wondered when you would find your way here, for it has the most spectacular view over the whole country-side."

She started at the sound of his voice and turned to look at him.

He thought now there was a wild look in her eyes that made him afraid.

He moved until he was near enough to hold on to her if necessary, and, forcing a smile to his lips, he continued:

"I am sure you came here because you could not sleep, as I have done since I was a boy."

She did not reply; instead, she turned her head away and once again looked down at the water.

There was silence until the Duke said quietly:

"It would be wrong, wicked, and a crime against life itself to do such a thing!"

He saw her stiffen, then in a voice he could hardly hear she replied:

"P-perhaps . . . like the prisoners . . . who you . . . told me about . . . there is no . . . alternative . . . At any rate . . . I cannot think of . . . one."

"Perhaps it would be easier if we talked about it to-gether."

She did not turn her head, and her long fair hair veiled the side of her face so that it was difficult for him to see her clearly.

He had the feeling she was listening as he said:

"One thing I have learned in my life is that however difficult things may seem, there is always hope."

"I . . . I think you are . . . over-optimistic."

"Once, when I was serving in the Army in the Sudan," the Duke went on, "we were besieged by some very unpleasant and ferocious natives after our ammunition and food had run out."

He could see she was listening, and continued:

"They were notorious for not taking prisoners, and I believed that it was only seconds before we all died."

He paused and after a moment, almost reluctantly, Vina asked:

"What . . . happened?"

"We were relieved at the last moment by a Squadron we had no idea was in the vicinity."

"You were . . . lucky," Vina said hesitatingly, "but for me . . . there is . . . no hope of a . . . S-squadron."

"How can you be sure of that?" the Duke asked. "And you know your father would not want you to be a coward."

She straightened herself.

Now she turned to look at him, her eyes very large and angry in the moonlight.

"I am *not* a coward!" she retorted. "And if I do die, I will be with Papa. He would understand."

"From all I have heard of your father," the Duke replied, "I do not believe he would give up until the very last minute."

Vina stared at him. Then when he thought she would

go on arguing with him, she said with a gesture that was somehow pathetic:

"What . . . am I . . . to do?"

"Shall we talk it over to-morrow?" the Duke suggested. "I am sure that together we can find a solution, as I suspect you will, with your father's help."

Somehow the moonlight was caught in her eyes as she said:

"If . . . Papa were here . . . he would . . . help me."

"Wherever he is," the Duke said quietly, "he will wish to do so."

She looked at him for a moment as if she could hardly believe what she had heard.

Then, in a voice a little above a whisper, she said:

"You are right! Of course you are right! It was wrong of me to come to the Tower of Despair."

"I should not have told you about it," the Duke said.

She took her hands from the battlements and he said:

"Now that we are here, look at the view. In the daytime you can see for nearly fifty miles. You have to admit it is very beautiful."

Vina did as he told her. Then she said as if it were a surprise:

"It *is* beautiful!"

It would have been impossible to say anything else about the stars above them and the moonlight turning the world to silver, and an unearthly beauty which caught at the Duke's heart.

"Yes, it is beautiful!" Vina said as though she were convincing herself, and at the same time she was surprised by what she saw.

"Could it be that in your longing for India," the Duke suggested, "you have not given England a chance?"

"I have not seen . . . anything as beautiful as . . . this before!"

"Perhaps you have not looked as hard as you should," he said. "To many people, especially those who live in the East, it means peace and security, and something which goes with them wherever they may be."

"I think . . . Papa sometimes . . . felt like that," Vina said.

"And he would want you to feel the same."

There was silence until the Duke said:

"I would not want you to catch cold, so I think we should go down; but remember what you have seen here and that this is England at its best."

"I . . . I will try," Vina said.

The Duke put out his hand and she put hers in his and he pulled her gently over the roof towards the door.

Her fingers were very cold. Yet he felt a certain vibration from them. It was different from anything he had felt before.

Then he told himself that all that mattered was that for the moment he had saved her from the Tower of Despair and that to-morrow they could talk it all over quietly.

Perhaps, although at this moment he could not think how, he would find a solution.

He was well aware from what he had seen of Lady Wallace that she would fight like a tiger to make sure that through Vina she was connected with Quarington.

If she ever knew what the girl intended, she would merely think she was being hysterical.

"I have to find some way to help Vina," the Duke

told himself as they reached the twisting steps of the Tower.

He let her go first so that he could shut the door and bolt it.

Then, as he saw her moving quickly down the twisting stone steps, he was forced, because his feet were larger, to move more slowly.

He also had to hold on to the sides because the steps were so narrow that he had to prevent himself from falling.

He had the feeling, however, that Vina floated down almost as if she had wings on her heels.

Finally he reached the door that led into the passage, and as he pulled it shut behind him he was aware that Vina was already vanishing ahead of him into the corridor.

Perhaps she would wait for him there. He thought it unconventional to ask her to come into the Sitting Room which adjoined his bedroom.

It would be wise, he thought, to talk to her and persuade her to be sensible.

At the same time, she might be shocked at such a suggestion.

Then, when he stepped into the corridor, he saw to his astonishment that Vina had not waited for him.

Instead, he caught a glimpse of her going through the door of her bedroom.

He was then aware that she had no wish to talk to him as any other woman he had known would have wanted to do.

He wondered for a split second whether he should call her. Then he knew it would cause a great deal of comment if anybody should hear him.

There was a *Boudoir* between General Alexander's room and Vina's, but nevertheless he felt it was something he should not risk.

He therefore walked down the corridor to his own Suite.

As he did so he thought that what had just happened was the most amazing thing he had ever known, something he could hardly credit.

He was aware that if Vina had thrown herself into the moat as she intended, it might have been a long time before they found her, and it would have caused a most unpleasant scandal.

He knew at any rate that he had prevented that from happening, but at the same time, the problem still remained.

If Vina Wallace felt so strongly about marrying his brother, how could he acquiesce to a marriage to avoid which she was prepared to die.

'I can give Edgar the money he wants,' the Duke thought, 'but if I do, surely, as the girl is so rich, this sort of situation will happen again and again.'

He also had the feeling that Lady Wallace would not give in so easily.

With an effort the Duke got into bed.

Two hours later he found that his brain was turning over and over the possibilities and the probabilities of the problem with which he had been presented.

"What can I do? What the devil can I do?" he asked.

There was no answer.

All he kept seeing was the stricken expression in Vina's eyes that he had seen at the Dining Room table.

chapter five

STRANGELY, because she had not expected to, Vina slept soundly, and when she awoke it was very much later than she had intended.

It meant that even if she had wished to, she would be too late to go to the stables before breakfast without encountering other members of the house-party.

She remembered a little belatedly that it was Sunday.

She thought she would like to go to Church to pray for some solution for her future.

She and her father had prayed in the buildings of many different religions—in Hindu and Buddhist Temples, in Muslim Mosques, and, when they were in the North, in strange monasteries inhabited by Tibetan monks.

Her mother had told her when she was young that it did not matter where one prayed. It was the prayer itself that counted, as long as it came from one's soul.

"I must go to Church!" Vina decided.

Her maid told her that there was a Communion Service at eight o'clock and she was sure that there would be nobody else in the party who would be there so early.

She put on her bonnet, which she tied under her chin with pink ribbons, and wore a shawl over her gown.

As soon as she knew what she intended, the maid had sent a message downstairs and Vina found an open carriage waiting for her outside the front door.

As she had expected, there was no one else to accompany her as she drove down the drive to the ancient Church which was situated just inside the Park gates.

There were very few people in the pews, and she thought most of them had come from the village.

The verger, realising she had arrived from the Big House, escorted her to the ducal pew, which was situated in the Chancel.

It was elaborately carved and there was a high reading desk in front of what seemed to be almost a throne. Vina knew it was for the Duke himself.

She knelt down on a red velvet hassock and prayed that God would help her escape from Lord Edgar and that her uncle would not force her to marry him.

She prayed until the Service started, then tried to find some answer for what she was asking, in the beautiful words of the prayers.

What they actually told her was that life was very precious and she had been wrong and wicked to try to throw it away.

She was afraid that her father would, as the Duke suggested, be ashamed of her, and she prayed for forgiveness not only from him but from God, who had given her life.

Yet, when the Service was over and she drove back to the house, she knew that the same question was repeating and repeating itself in her mind:

'How can I go on living if I have to marry Lord Edgar?'

There was some surprise among the guests at breakfast when they realised she was late because she had been to Church.

"Of all the people in this party who I am sure have no sins to confess," one man said to her, "it is you, Miss Wallace!"

"I wish that were true," Vina replied.

He smiled at her flirtatiously.

"Tell me what is your most besetting sin?" he asked. "It cannot be Vanity, for you appear quite unconscious of your beauty."

Vina knew it was a compliment, so she answered demurely:

"My sins are ... private ... as I am sure ... yours are!"

Several of his friends laughed at this, and said jokingly:

"Not as private as all that! But we will not sneak on you, Harry!"

"I shall be extremely annoyed if you do!" he replied. "I want Miss Wallace to think of me as a White Knight, ready to defend her against all her enemies."

Again there was laughter, and Vina thought miserably that there was no Knight to save her from the dragon who had the face of Lord Edgar.

He came in to the Dining Room just as she had risen from her place to leave, and when she walked towards the door went ahead to open it for her.

She thanked him without looking at him, then realised, as she stepped into the hall, that he had followed her.

"I want to talk to you, Miss Wallace."

"There is . . . nothing to . . . say," she answered.

"I have a lot to say," he replied, "and I insist on your hearing me."

It was impossible to run away from him when there were two footmen on duty in the hall, and she had the frightened feeling that if she tried to do so he would hold on to her.

She therefore walked beside him down the corridor until he opened the door of a Sitting Room she had not been in before.

It was a small room, exquisitely furnished with Louis XIV furniture, and pictures by Fragonard and Boucher on the walls.

Vina's heart was pounding frantically because she was frightened and her lips felt dry.

But, as Lord Edgar shut the door, she lifted her chin and told herself she would not let him see how frightened she was.

Yet, because she felt her legs could hardly support her, she sat down on an upright chair.

As she expected, he stood in front of her with his back to the fire.

"First," he said, and he was speaking to her in a different voice from what he had used before, "I feel I should apologise."

"N-no . . . please . . ." Vina pleaded.

However, he continued as if she had not spoken:

"I had no idea until you told me that the plot hatched

96

between your uncle and my brother had not your approval."

Vina did not speak, and he said in quite a considerable tone:

"What I said must have been a shock."

"Yes . . . it was!" Vina murmured. "I had no . . . idea that that was . . . why we had been . . . invited to stay . . . here."

There was silence, then Lord Edgar said:

"Now that you have had time to understand what has been planned, I hope you will view things differently and that we can try to make our marriage more or less successful."

Vina clasped her fingers together so tightly that it hurt.

Then she said in a voice that she tried to make calm:

"I know what you are saying is what my uncle and aunt wish to happen. At the same time, please understand that it is . . . impossible for me to . . . marry anyone I do not . . . love."

"That is what you said yesterday," Lord Edgar replied, "but you must be aware that marriages are always arranged amongst the aristocracy."

There was a little pause after Lord Edgar said the word "aristocracy."

Vina was aware that he was going to say "and even among people like yourself," because he considered her not as important as he was.

It was insulting, but she was aware that he was trying to be conciliatory and there was no use her taking offence openly.

What he had to understand was that she could not and would not marry him.

"What I am going to suggest," Lord Edgar continued as she did not speak, "is that we accept the inevitable without recrimination and try to make the best of—"

Again he stopped and Vina, reading his thoughts, knew he was thinking of saying: The best of a bad job.

He however deftly turned it into:

"The best for us both."

He looked at her enquiringly as he did so.

It was, she thought, as if for the first time he was noticing her as an individual and considering her good points in the same way a man would inspect a horse before he bought it.

"Because you are young and have lived only in the country," he went on, "I feel sure you will find a great deal to amuse you in London. We can certainly afford a bigger house than I have at the moment, in which case, you can entertain all your friends."

"I have no friends . . . in London," Vina said.

There was a twist to Lord Edgar's lips as he replied:

"That will be remedied once you are one of the family."

Again there was silence. Then he said, as if the question were uppermost in his mind:

"All we have to do is to announce our engagement, and once that is made public, there will be no need for our marriage to be hurried, as I suggested yesterday."

Vina drew in her breath.

She knew that if their marriage were announced as he suggested, it would soon be discovered how rich she was.

Then his creditors would be only too ready to wait for the money he owed them.

She thought she could see only too clearly how he

had reasoned this out. If not by himself, then he had listened to somebody with more intelligence than he had.

He had it all settled, she thought, and once again she was aware that she was trapped and there was little she could do about it.

Then, although she was frightened and it was difficult to breathe, she felt as if her father were beside her, telling her what to say.

In a voice which sounded controlled, she managed to answer:

"As . . . this has been such a . . . surprise, My Lord, I should be grateful if I could have a . . . little time to . . . think it over and that we need not say . . . anything to my uncle and aunt until we have . . . talked about it . . . again."

She sensed as she spoke that Lord Edgar heaved a sigh of relief because he thought he had won.

He replied eagerly, almost too eagerly:

"Of course—if that is what you want, Miss Wallace. Or should I say Vina? I am only too ready to agree."

He smiled before he added:

"As I understand you will be leaving to-morrow, perhaps you could give me your decision and we can talk about it to my brother and, of course, to your uncle before luncheon."

"Yes . . . we can do . . . that," Vina said.

Lord Edgar moved closer, and she had the terrifying feeling that he might be going to kiss her.

She rose quickly to her feet, saying as she did so:

"Please . . . will you keep everything . . . secret until . . . then? I think, therefore, it is a . . . mistake for us to be . . . here alone."

She did not wait for his reply, but hurried to the door. Only as she reached it did Lord Edgar say:

"We will talk about it to-morrow after breakfast here in this room. Is that agreed?"

"Yes," Vina answered, and felt it was impossible to say any more.

She hurried upstairs and was walking along the corridor to her bedroom, when she met her uncle coming down to breakfast.

"Good-morning, Uncle Alexander!" she said, kissing him on the cheek.

"Good-morning, Vina! I am afraid I am rather late."

"I am sure there is plenty of breakfast left for you," she said, trying to smile.

"I think your aunt wants to talk to you," the General said, and started to descend the stairs.

Vina hurried into her own room.

The one thing she wanted to avoid was a confrontation with her aunt.

She had realised yesterday evening that Lady Wallace had come to her bedroom after she had locked her door and then gone away because she thought she must be asleep.

She had skilfully avoided talking to her aunt before dinner but had known that she had later peeped into her room after she was in bed.

When she had found the room in darkness, Lady Wallace had shut the door quietly and gone away again.

"I cannot talk to her. There will only be a scene when I tell her I have not yet decided what to do about Lord Edgar."

She also knew that if she told her aunt they were going to talk about everything to-morrow morning, she would be unable to keep the information to herself.

Inevitably, she would chatter to the other ladies in the party, and perhaps also to the Duke.

'I must just avoid her,' Vina thought.

She therefore did not go into her bedroom but waited until her uncle had entered the Breakfast Room.

Then she slipped down the stairs.

She made her way to the Library and, collecting some books, climbed up to the balcony.

At the far end of it there was a seat which was low and comfortable, and she was aware that unless anyone on the floor below looked very carefully, she could not be seen.

She opened her book and thought she would keep out of sight until luncheon time.

But for once the written word did not capture and enchant her as it usually did.

Instead, she felt that all she could see on the open pages was the face of Lord Edgar.

Although she tried to stop herself from being uncharitable, she knew how greedy he was for her money and that he actively disliked her as a woman because she was to be his wife.

She had known, too, when he was speaking to her in what she knew was a deliberately quiet and reasonable manner, that he had hated the effort he had to make.

He was obviously thinking that the sacrifice was worthwhile if it meant that he could get his hands on her fortune.

She was aware as he smiled at her that he was still as puzzled as he had been on the previous day, when he had shocked and had frightened her with his aggressive approach.

She thought everything about him was unpleasant, and she knew with an unmistakable conviction that once she was his wife, he would treat her despicably.

"What can I do, Papa?" she asked. Now, once again, she was desperately afraid.

She stayed in the Library for a long time. Then suddenly below her she heard the door open and somebody come in.

She sank a little lower on the seat to ensure that whoever it was was not aware she was there.

Then she heard Lord Edgar's voice say rather sharply:

"We can talk in here. What was it you wanted to say to me?"

"I thought it wise to make sure we were not overheard," a man's voice replied.

He was an older person, whom Vina knew had been introduced to her as Sir Robert Warde, and whom she had sat opposite at dinner.

She had not noticed, while he was flirting with a lady sitting next to him, that he had drunk a great deal and that the servants were continually filling up his glass.

"You must be aware of what I am going to say," he now said to Lord Edgar. "It is that the ten thousand pounds you owe me is long overdue, and I do not suppose you wish me to appeal to your brother?"

Lord Edgar laughed, and it was not a particularly pleasant sound.

"I think as you are an intelligent man, Robert," he replied, "you must have some idea why that young woman, Vina Wallace, was included in this house-party?"

There was a little pause. Then Sir Robert said:

"Good heavens! We were talking in the Smoking Room about her having an enormous fortune. Are you telling me you are going to marry the girl?"

"Of course I am," Lord Edgar replied. "I would be a damned fool to let an opportunity like that pass me by."

"My dear boy, I had no idea! Is she really as rich as they say she is?"

"Apparently some Indian Prince left her father a few million," Lord Edgar replied, "but as he is dead, and there are no other children, she has inherited the lot!"

"Then I must congratulate you! I never thought you would be so intelligent as to marry an heiress to get out of your difficulties."

"That is what I intend to do," Lord Edgar said, "and, of course, Robert, the moment the knot is tied, you shall be paid what you are owed as well as everybody else who has been dunning me!"

Now his voice was rude and sarcastic, and Sir Robert said:

"Now, do not take up that attitude, Edgar. We have known each other a long time, and I have been a good friend."

"I am not prepared to argue about that," Lord Edgar replied.

"When you receive your golden *rupees*," Sir Robert said reflectively, "I hope you will not forget your old friends."

"I am not likely to do that," Lord Edgar said, "and let me assure you, Robert, things will be exactly the same as they have always been."

"Well, Connie will be pleased about that!"

"I intend to give her the finest diamonds any little 'Cyprian' has ever possessed."

"And what about your wife? What will she say?"

"I will give her plenty of babies to keep her busy," Lord Edgar replied, and they both laughed.

"If there is one thing about you, Edgar," Sir Robert Warde said, "it is that you always manage, in one way or another, to extricate yourself from trouble."

"This time more successfully than usual," Lord Edgar said with satisfaction, "and as you are going to be paid with interest, let us have a drink on it."

"I am very, very pleased about that," Sir Robert Warde said, "and do not forget to ask me to the first riotous party you give after you are married; that is, if your wife is not playing hostess."

"Connie will do that," Lord Edgar said, "and you can bring Lulu or have the first pick of the best of the 'soiled doves' that I can collect together."

"That is what I want to hear," Sir Robert replied. "Now, come on, my boy! Where is that drink?"

The two men were laughing as they went from the Library.

Vina was staring ahead, and the stricken look which the Duke had seen in her eyes the previous night was intensified.

As it happened, she knew who Connie was.

She had come into the Drawing-Room rather quietly about a month before and heard Lady Farringham say to her aunt:

"I am told Lord Edgar is spending a fortune, which he does not possess, on that young actress who appears at the Olympic Theatre."

"Is that the same one who cost him so much last year?" Lady Warde asked.

"Oh, no!" Lady Farringham had replied. "Connie

Courtney was then under the protection of the Earl of Hastings, who I have always thought was a terrible old man, although, of course, very rich. Now it appears that Lord Edgar has inveigled her away and the parties he gives for her are worse than any orgy ever thought up by the Romans!"

The two ladies had laughed, but Vina, thinking such gossip was boring, had slipped away to another room, where she could read.

Now she remembered what had been said.

How could she allow money to be spent on women who she was aware no Lady would know?

She had thought of the children she had seen starving in India and the poverty, which she knew because she read the newspapers, that existed also in England.

She felt it was an insult to her father that the fortune that had been left to him should be expended in such an outrageous manner.

"How can I stop it? What can I do?" she asked. There was no answer.

After a time, because she could no longer concentrate, she put the books back on the shelves from which she had taken them and slipped out of the house by a side door into the garden.

As the Duke had made her realise the night before, the surroundings of Quarington were very beautiful.

There were not only distant views, there were also the spring shrubs coming into bloom in the garden, daffodils under the trees, and the green lawns which ended in a water-garden.

There was a small cascade falling over some rocks, ending in a huge pool which later would be filled with water lilies.

It was all very beautiful.

Because it was unprecedentedly warm for the time of year, she walked among the trees not realising she had come without a shawl or a bonnet.

The budding leaves on the trees had a special beauty of their own and Vina thought that in a month or so there would be a blaze of blossom. It would seem like Fairyland.

Then she remembered that by that time, unless she had saved herself, she would be married to a man whom she hated and despised.

Her whole body shrank in horror at the idea of being his wife.

"Save me, save me!" she cried to the trees towering above her, the flowers growing at her feet, and the distant view which last night had been enchanted by the moonlight.

Then, suddenly, as if somebody were speaking to her—she was sure it was her father—she knew what she must do.

* * *

"Surely," Lady Wallace said to her husband, "he has spoken to Vina by this time?"

They were somewhat detached from the party which had left the Dining Room and were moving into one of the State Reception Rooms.

Lady Wallace spoke in a very low voice, but the General looked round a little nervously as if he felt she might be overheard.

"There is no hurry," he said.

"But we are leaving to-morrow," Lady Wallace protested, "and once they are engaged, there is so much for us to discuss with the dear Duke."

The General was prevented from replying because at that moment the Duke came up to them.

"I was wondering, Lady Wallace," he said, "what you and your husband would like to do this afternoon? I do not know whether you have yet seen the Picture Gallery, or if you would prefer to go driving."

"I am waiting to hear what dear little Vina is doing," Lady Wallace replied in dulcet tones.

The Duke looked round and realised that since they had left the Dining Room she had disappeared.

His brother was talking to two men. The conversation was obviously very amusing, as they were all laughing.

"I do not want any of my guests to do anything but enjoy themselves," he said, "and perhaps the wisest thing a host can do in these circumstances is to leave them alone."

"Oh, no, Your Grace! I am sure everybody wants to be with you!" Lady Wallace exclaimed flatteringly.

"Well, I personally am going to the stables," the Duke said.

He moved away as he spoke, and instantly Irene Halford was at his side.

"Dearest Alveric!" she said. "Will you take me driving, or could we have a cosy chat in my *Boudoir?*"

"I am afraid, Irene, I have to look after my guests," the Duke answered. "We could go driving, but it would be a mistake for you to be with me as you were yesterday."

Lady Halford pouted petulantly; then she said in the soft and seductive tones he knew so well:

"I will go and lie down and you shall join me as soon as you can."

The Duke knew exactly what she meant, but merely replied:

"I will do what I can, Irene, but I have no wish to lose my reputation for being a good host."

He walked away from her and with difficulty she prevented herself from stamping her foot.

She had been so sure, when he had asked her to stay for the weekend because he knew her husband was away, that she had captured him completely.

She thought that he was, as she had always wanted, overwhelmingly in love with her.

Yet, there was no doubt that at the moment he was being elusive. It was something she did not like.

She had noticed with satisfaction when she arrived that there were no rivals in the party.

The other women were either accompanied by their husbands or else were too insignificant to compete with her beauty or her wit.

Now, because the Duke was not so attentive or so ardent as she wanted him to be, she was determined to redouble her attraction for him.

She would make him completely a captive of her love.

"He is so handsome!" she told herself. "I will kill any woman who tries to take him from me!"

* * *

Vina had once again found her way to the Library.

She thought that judging by her experience in the morning she was unlikely to find anyone there. If anybody did enter the Library, they would not see her.

She took out the books she had put away earlier, climbed up the twisting steps to the balcony, and sat down in the same place she had been before.

Now, because she had made an important decision, she was able to concentrate on what she was reading.

Nearly an hour later she did not hear the Library door open, nor did she realise that anybody had climbed onto the balcony until she looked up to see the Duke standing in front of her.

"I thought you would be hiding here!" he said.

"How can . . . you have . . . thought that?"

"Because I knew you would want to read and also you would want to be alone," he replied.

"Your books are very . . . exciting!"

"I was sure they would please you. Now, Vina, suppose we have a little talk, as you promised me you would last night?"

He did not sit down beside her as she expected, although it would have been rather a squeeze.

Instead, to her surprise, he sat down on the floor with his back against a bookcase, his feet stretched out against the balcony.

It made him seem less overwhelming and in a way more human, and as she thought of it, she knew it was what he intended.

"Last night you frightened me," the Duke said, "and it was only when you had left me, much sooner than I intended, that I realised I had not asked you to give me your word of honour that it was something you would not do again."

He paused, and when she did not speak, he said:

"I am waiting to have it now."

"As I told you . . . I have no . . . wish to be a coward," Vina said hesitatingly.

"In which case, swear to me on everything in which you believe that you will not again attempt to take your life," the Duke said.

"I . . . swear to you," Vina said in a very low voice, "that I will not throw myself from . . . the Tower of Despair."

It flashed through the Duke's mind that there were other ways of committing suicide.

But, as he thought it would be a mistake to pressure Vina in any way, he felt he must be content with her promise.

"Now," he said, "shall we talk about your future?"

Again there was a little pause. Then Vina said:

"Could we . . . please leave it until to-morrow? I am trying to . . . think clearly and what Papa would have called 'logically.' Everything has been such a . . . shock that it is . . . difficult to be . . . constructive."

She spoke as if she were thinking out every word, and after a moment the Duke said:

"I want to tell you, Vina, that I think you are a very intelligent, very unusual, and indeed remarkable young woman."

He spoke with a note of sincerity that made her blush. Then she asked:

"Would it be possible . . . while everybody else is busy . . . for me to ride Hercules again for—"

She stopped, and the Duke looked at her questioningly.

He had the feeling she had been going to say: For the last time.

He told himself it would be a great mistake at this

particular moment when he thought she was perhaps becoming used to the idea of marrying Edgar for him to submit her to any sort of inquisition.

He smiled before he replied:

"I think, if we are clever, we can slip out through a side door which I shall show you when you are ready. Nobody will know where we have gone, and although it is a great sacrifice on my part, I will allow you to ride Hercules."

Vina's eyes lit up and she gave a little laugh that was like that of a child being promised a very special treat.

The Duke rose to his feet and they climbed down from the balcony.

Then, because he thought they might be seen if they went through the hall, he took her up to the first floor by the secondary staircase.

He told her where to meet him, and Vina was sure that nobody had any idea where they were going before they reached the stables.

After the grooms had saddled the horses at a record speed, they set off in the same direction by which Vina had travelled the day before towards the flat land beyond the paddock.

The Duke was riding a stallion that was nearly as impressive as Hercules, but a little older.

Because he had ridden him for two years, he responded to his every wish.

Hercules was, as usual, obstreperous.

The Duke was confident now that Vina could control him.

He thought, too, it would have been impossible for any woman to look more alluring than she did with her slight figure, riding such an enormous animal.

He was also aware that there were stars of happiness in her eyes, a very different expression from the stricken look which had perturbed him the night before.

Nearly an hour had passed when he said:

"I think we should turn for home."

Vina looked suddenly serious, and there was a dreamy note in her voice as she said:

"Yesterday ... when I reached here ... I thought I should return ... but I really wanted to go on riding ... forever into the far horizon where ... there would be no ... problems and no ... difficulties."

"Have you ever considered that life would be very dull without them?" the Duke asked. "You told me that you found England monotonous. Perhaps that was because you had not yet faced a challenge."

He thought as he spoke that he was trying to make her marriage sound exciting.

Instead, he knew, if he were honest, that for anyone so sensitive, it would be a living hell.

"I ought to save her," he told himself.

Then, as she turned Hercules's head, she looked at him with an unexpectedly mischievous expression in her eyes.

Before he could stop her, she had ridden the horse towards the high fence she had jumped when she had been running away from him.

"No, Vina, no!" he said sharply, but it was too late.

Vina had already taken Hercules over it and was riding confidently onto the next, and there was nothing the Duke could do but follow her.

Only as he caught up with her after the third fence had been taken did she ask in a small, childlike voice which he found particularly attractive:

"Are you . . . angry with . . . me?"

"No, only astonished," he replied.

"That I can ride Hercules, or that I should have the . . . impudence to . . . defy you?"

"Both! At the same time, I realise that my fears for your safety are unfounded. How can you have learnt to ride so brilliantly?"

"I have ridden in some very odd places with Papa," she answered, "and sometimes we had to escape from unpleasant situations, besides finding our way across country without maps or compass."

"Then I know your father would be proud of his pupil," the Duke said.

"You told me last night that I should not do anything of which he would disapprove," Vina said quietly.

"I am quite sure he would want you to be brave and ready to face an enemy with determination and courage."

He hoped as he spoke that he did not sound too much as if he were preaching.

Vina did not reply.

He was, however, sure as they rode on that he had convinced her although they had not actually discussed it, that her marriage to Edgar would be a challenge.

They did not speak as they trotted back towards the stables.

The grooms were waiting for them, and when Vina dismounted she patted Hercules and kissed him on the nose.

"Good-bye!" the Duke heard her whisper.

He wondered as they walked towards the side door whether there was any inner meaning in her farewell.

Then he told himself he was being imaginative.

There was no equivalent of the French *"Au revoir"* in the English language, and "Good-bye" could mean parting of a few hours as well as a farewell for eternity.

"Thank you, Your Grace," Vina said as they stopped at the bottom of the stairs. "Thank you . . . for a wonderful . . . experience I shall never . . . forget!"

The Duke did not reply and she ran up the stairs.

He stood watching until she was out of sight.

Then, as he walked towards the Great Hall, he found himself wondering once again how he could find a way to save Vina from marrying his brother.

chapter six

AT dinner the Duke thought Vina certainly looked much happier than she had the night before.

She was talking animatedly to the men on either side of her, and it struck him that Edgar also seemed in a better humour.

It flashed through his mind that they might have come to some secret arrangement between themselves. Then it seemed impossible.

He had, however, no chance of talking to Vina after dinner, as she did not play the piano again.

She disappeared almost like a ghost before he was aware what she intended to do.

He knew that her aunt was very annoyed at her disappearance.

He sat down beside her on the sofa while his other guests were arranging themselves at the card tables, and Lady Wallace said:

"I cannot imagine why Vina should be so elusive, unless, of course, she is with your brother."

The Duke looked round the room and saw that Edgar had also vanished.

He had the idea, however, that once again he had gone to the Billiard Room, where he spent as much time drinking as playing Billiards.

He thought, however, that it would be a mistake to get into a confidential conversation with Lady Wallace and merely said:

"There is plenty of time for everybody to talk things over. Let me find you a place at the card tables."

He seemed to make it an order, and Lady Wallace obediently sat down to play Bridge with three of the older members of the party.

The Duke was curious enough to go to the Billiard Room to see if Edgar was there.

He had not been mistaken.

His brother was in the Billiard Room, watching his opponent play, holding a cue in one hand and a glass of port in the other.

Without making himself obvious, the Duke returned to the Drawing Room, only to find, as he expected, that there was no sign of Vina.

For the rest of the evening Lady Halford refused to leave his side and he thought, when he said good-night to the General, that his wife looked at him reproachfully.

'There is nothing I can say,' he thought to himself, 'and doubtless before they leave to-morrow something will have been settled one way or the other.'

He was, however, very surprised when Sir Robert

Warde, coming up behind him, stopped him on the first landing and said:

"I am exceedingly glad to hear the good news about Edgar, and you must be delighted!"

The Duke frowned, thinking it was typical of his brother that, if he were engaged to Vina Wallace, he would have to hear it at first from an outsider.

He did not know Sir Robert Warde well, but they had met on many a racecourse, and he had asked him this weekend because he was a good Bridge player.

They had, in fact, been talking together at White's Club when he was planning his house party.

Now Sir Robert was obviously waiting for him to reply, and he said after a moment:

"I imagine that anything my brother has told you has not been discussed amongst the family; it is a secret."

"I expect that is true," Sir Robert said, "but between you and me, Quarington, Edgar owes me a great deal of money and I shall be glad to have it back in my pocket."

There was something in the way Warde spoke which told the Duke that he was trying to ingratiate himself because of his generosity.

He decided that Warde would not be his guest again.

"Good-night, Sir Robert!" he said. "I hope you have everything you want."

"Everything!"

Sir Robert would have continued the conversation had the Duke not moved quickly away and gone down the corridor towards his own room.

For some inexplicable reason he did not visit Lady Halford that night.

He knew she would be extremely angry, and also perturbed by his absence.

But he wanted to think about Edgar and Vina. Quite unexpectedly, he had no desire to make love to her.

Because of his previous experience with women who, once they had fallen in love with him, cast discretion to the winds, he locked his door.

Then, before he got into bed, he pulled back the curtains.

He lay looking at the stars and the moonlight, which the night before had made the view from the Tower an enchanted Fairyland.

He tried not to think of the moment when he had seen Vina looking down at the moat and had known that she intended to throw herself into it.

If she had been missing the following morning, he would not have imagined for one second that she would do anything so incredible.

She was young, she was very beautiful, and enormously rich.

Most people would say she had everything in the world that any woman could want.

Then he thought of his brother and how, despite his handsome looks, how coarse and debauched he was.

He understood what Vina was feeling about him, or rather, he told himself, what she had felt.

This afternoon, when he talked to her on the balcony in the Library, the terror had gone from her eyes.

There was also something calm about her that had not been there before.

He had the feeling that he was being rather obtuse, and it annoyed him.

He prided himself on understanding people and the perception he had about them.

It was very difficult for them to deceive him.

Yet, as he turned everything over in his mind, he was quite certain he was missing some vital explanation for Vina's attitude and what Sir Robert Warde had just told him.

If it was true that after all that had happened she intended to marry Edgar, why had she not confided in him?

He found himself calculating that there had been just enough time for them to see each other before dinner.

Then he told himself he was being ridiculous.

Everything was working out just as it had been planned by the General and Lady Wallace. He had concurred with the plan. Why should he trouble himself over it?

He found, as he lay awake looking at the stars and the moonlight, that the mystery of Vina would not allow him to sleep.

Finally, just before dawn came, he fell into an uneasy slumber, then awoke with a start to find it was nearly seven o'clock.

Now, he remembered, he had forgotten to tell his valet to call him early.

This meant that he would not be wakened properly for another half-hour.

He decided that he could not lie in bed being confronted by the same problems which had kept him awake for so many hours the previous night.

He rose and unlocked the door, then rang for his valet, Hodgson, who had been with him, like John Simpson, when he was in the Army.

They had fought together many times, and, on one occasion, had very nearly died together.

There was therefore an affinity between them, different from the usual one between master and servant.

He had washed and shaved, and was getting dressed before Hodgson came into the room. Somewhat unnecessarily he remarked:

"You're up early, Your Grace!"

"I know, Hodgson," the Duke replied. "It is a nice morning, and I want to be out riding."

He thought as he spoke that if Vina had gone to the stables as early as she had on Saturday morning, by now she would be a long way from the house.

He was, however, quite certain he could find her.

Looking exceedingly smart in his whipcloth riding coat and his boots polished so that they shone like mirrors, he walked quickly down the corridor.

Only when he reached Vina's room did he hesitate.

He wondered if he should knock and find out if she had overslept as he had, and would want to come riding with him.

Then he saw, beside the door, there was a letter.

It was lying on one of the exquisite French Commodes which decorated this part of the house.

As he glanced at it he saw that it was addressed to himself.

He picked it up quickly, opened it, and found the letter consisted of two separate pages. He read:

Please do not be angry with me, but I cannot marry Lord Edgar. I will keep my promise to you, and not be a coward. At the same time, I cannot marry someone I do not and never could love.

I have therefore gone to stay with friends, who will look after me.

Please do not let Uncle Alexander try to find

me, and see that the letter enclosed reaches his Solicitors.

Thank you for your kindness and for letting me ride Hercules. I shall never forget him, or Quarington.

Vina

The Duke drew in his breath; then he read the second page.

Messrs. Redbridge, Robinson, and Metcalfe,

Dear Sirs:

Kindly pay Lord Edgar Quary the sum of 50,000 pounds. His Grace, the Duke of Quarington, will make it clear that this is my wish, and that my intention must not be overruled by my Guardian, General Sir Alexander Wallace.

Yours truly,
Vina Wallace.

The Duke put both letters into his pocket and ran down the stairs.

He sent a servant for the night-footman, who had already left the hall and ordered a maid who was cleaning out the fireplace to find John Simpson.

Then he went into his Study and read both letters again before the night-footman was ushered into the room.

"You were on duty last night, James?"

"Yes, Y'Grace."

"Did you see Miss Wallace?"

"Yes, Y'Grace."

"Tell me exactly what happened."

"'Er come down the stairs about four o'clock, Y'Grace."

"What did she do?"

"'Er asked me to go t'the stables an' order a carriage for to go roun' t'the side door. I jus' done as 'er tells me, Y'Grace."

"Yes, yes, of course," the Duke agreed. "What happened then?"

"Well, a'ter I done that, 'er tells I to bring down 'er trunks. There were two o' them, Y'Grace."

"She drove away alone?"

"Yes, Y'Grace."

"Where did she drive to?"

"Oi thinks it be th' station, Y'Grace."

"The station?" the Duke repeated in surprise.

"Yes, Y'Grace."

At that moment John Simpson, who had obviously been only half dressed when the Duke sent for him, came hurrying into the Study.

"You sent for me?" he asked apprehensively as he saw the night-footman.

"You may go now, James," the Duke said, "but do not talk of what has occurred—do you understand? Keep it to yourself."

"Yes, Y'Grace."

The door shut behind him and John Simpson looked enquiringly at the Duke, who said sharply:

"Vina Wallace has run away! At four o'clock she ordered James to fetch a carriage to the side door to take her to the station."

"Then she will have caught the Milk Train," John Simpson said.

"The Milk Train?" the Duke enquired.

"That is what it is always called because it picks up the milk from the various farms in the vicinity and reaches London a little after six o'clock."

The Duke looked at the clock on the mantelpiece. Then he said:

"Where is she likely to go? She told me she had no friends in London."

"I suppose Lady Wallace would know."

"The last thing we want to do at the moment is to tell Lady Wallace what has happened!" the Duke said decisively.

John Simpson nodded in agreement. Then he said:

"Perhaps she was trying to find somewhere to stay."

"What do you mean by that?" the Duke asked.

"Just before luncheon I overheard her asking one of the footmen to fetch Saturday's *Times*. It seemed an unusual paper to interest a young girl."

"The Times!" the Duke said reflectively.

"Send the maid who looks after her to me, and try if you can, John, to keep everybody in the house from chatting about this."

"I think that is impossible!" John Simpson replied as he left the room.

The maid, looking nervous, came into the Duke's Study two minutes later.

As she shut the door behind her she dropped the Duke a curtsy, and said in a voice that quivered:

"You wanted me, Your Grace?"

"It is Gladys, is it not?"

"Yes, Your Grace."

"I want you to tell me if you have any idea, Gladys, why Miss Wallace should have left us so very early this morning."

"I've no idea, Your Grace. It was quite a shock when I goes into her room this morning to find her not there, and all her things gone!"

"Did she pack them herself?" the Duke enquired.

"Oh, no, Your Grace. She tells me yesterday evening to pack them all ready before she comes to bed just in case her uncle wished to leave soon after breakfast this morning."

"So she took everything she possessed with her."

"Yes, Your Grace, two trunks and her jewel-case."

The Duke was not surprised at that.

It was unlikely that any woman would leave behind such magnificent jewels as he had seen Lady Wallace showing to Irene Halford and to two other women in the party.

He had gone into the Morning Room and found them almost drooling over them. He realised that they could have come only from the East.

He had not been particularly interested and had just glanced at the huge emeralds that had been set in necklaces and bracelets surrounded with diamonds.

He had also seen the rubies which he was well aware were worth a King's ransom.

His guests were trying the rings on their fingers and the bracelets on their wrists.

The Duke thought somewhat cynically that most women would give their bodies and their hearts to any man who could produce such treasures.

"Vina is a very lucky girl!" Lady Wallace had said to him.

He walked away because he disliked the expression of greed in her voice, and on the face of Irene Halford.

He knew quite well that the latter was thinking that she should be rewarded in a similar manner for the love she had given him.

It made him think that all women were prostitutes at heart.

The cynical lines on his face deepened, and he went out of the house as if in need of fresh air.

Now it struck him that if Vina had taken the jewels with her and was travelling unattended, she might find herself in serious trouble.

Realising that Gladys was still waiting, he asked:

"Miss Wallace left nothing behind her?"

"Nothin', Your Grace. The room was quite empty, except for a book Miss Wallace had taken from the Library. About India, it was, an' she was readin' all the time I was dressin' her for dinner last night."

"That will be all, thank you, Gladys," the Duke said. "Ask Mr. Simpson to come in."

He knew John Simpson would be waiting outside. It was easier for him to talk to the servants without his being there.

As he came into the room, the Duke asked quickly:

"What is the time of the next train to London?"

John Simpson looked at the clock.

"There will be one in just over an hour."

"I will catch it!" the Duke said. "And see that I have plenty of money—and my passport and Saturday's *Times*."

"Your passport?" John Simpson ejaculated.

But the Duke had already left the room and did not hear him.

Upstairs, as he expected, he found that Hodgson was still tidying his room, and gave him his orders.

Because he was used to the Duke expecting everything to be done at the double, Hodgson packed two trunks, which were already on the carriage when the Duke came out of the side door where no one would see him leave.

"Do not tell anyone in the party what has occurred," he said to John Simpson, who was beside him, "except, of course, for General and Lady Wallace, and swear them to secrecy. And tell Lord Edgar as little as possible. He will only talk, and that would be a great mistake."

"I only hope you are right in your supposition as to where Miss Wallace has gone," John Simpson said.

"I will know as soon as we reach London," the Duke answered.

He had driven off, and when the carriage was out of sight, John Simpson walked into the house, feeling that he did not relish the explanations that lay ahead of him.

*   *   *

The Duke travelled to London in an Express Train which stopped at Quarington Halt only when a signal which was worked by the guests themselves brought it to a standstill.

Otherwise there were no stops until it reached Paddington.

There had been no time to arrange for the Duke's own carriage to be waiting for him outside the station.

Hodgson found them a cab with what appeared to be a reasonably fast horse.

They drove through London quicker than might have

been expected. At Fenchurch Station the Duke learnt that the Boat Train had left two hours before and that there was a wait of nearly three-quarters of an hour for the next one.

When the Duke received *The Times* of the previous Saturday, he looked at the "Sailings" on the back page.

As he expected, a ship of the Peninsular and Oriental Shipping Line was leaving Tilbury Landing Stage that day.

It would sail on the afternoon tide, the time of which varied, and he thought he would be lucky if he reached Tilbury in time.

He was quite sure, because his intuition told him so, that Vina would be on board the S.S. *Magnificent*.

As he thought it over, he remembered his conversation with her about India and how much it meant to her.

He was completely sure that as she had promised him she would not destroy herself, the only way of escape was for her to run away.

Because she loved not only India, but also the Indian people, she would feel safe amongst them.

Also, with her jewels to support her, she would not be an encumbrance to whoever she stayed with.

She would certainly be able to pay for anything she required.

Yet, at the same time, it was inconceivable that any Lady, especially one so young and attractive as Vina, should travel alone without getting into all sorts of trouble.

If it was known she was carrying such valuable jewels, she would undoubtedly be robbed.

The Duke, thinking of her and the fear he had seen in

her large eyes, felt that the train carrying him towards Tilbury was inordinately slow.

He was also afraid that for once his intuition might have failed him and that she would not be on board the S.S. *Magnificent* when he reached her.

'If I am mistaken, God knows where I can look next,' he thought.

He was appalled at the thought of Vina wondering about London alone.

He arrived at Tilbury and, springing from the train almost before it came to a standstill and leaving Hodgson to cope with the luggage, he went to the new P. & O. Office which was at the entrance to the docks.

"I wish to be a passenger aboard the S.S. *Magnificent*," he said to the man in charge.

"I think you've missed her, Sir," the clerk replied.

The Duke looked through the glass window as he spoke, saw the seamen were just casting the ropes off the bollards, and knew it was only a question of minutes before the gangways were pulled aboard.

He threw a number of notes down on the desk and said:

"I have to catch that ship."

Then he was running, followed by Hodgson and two porters, who pulled his baggage on a truck.

They reached the gangway just as it was being lifted.

With a wild scramble the Duke, Hodgson, and the baggage were on board, only a few seconds before the ship began to move.

There were a number of passengers leaning over the rails watching his arrival, but the Duke felt sure that Vina would not be amongst them.

If she was, however, there would be nothing she could do to escape from him.

Breathless, he began to climb up the companion way, and only as he reached the Purser's Office did he remember that he was travelling incognito.

He never used his Ducal title, which invariably encouraged journalists and gossips, but travelled as Lord Elverton, another of his names.

The Purser was a large, fat, and very affable man and, as the Duke introduced himself, he said:

"You cut it a bit fine, My Lord."

"I knew only at the last moment that my journey was imperative," the Duke replied grandly, "and I want the best accommodation with which you can provide me."

There were no Suites on the P. & O. Liners, but the Duke knew of old how comfortable a passage could be if one could afford it.

He therefore took two of the largest and best cabins, unoccupied because they were so expensive, and gave orders that one should be turned into a Sitting Room.

He also took a cabin for Hodgson as near as possible to his own, and, when everything had been arranged, he said casually:

"May I look at the Passenger List?"

"Of course, My Lord," the Purser replied, "but there are two passengers who, like yourself, were too late to be included on it."

"Two?" the Duke queried.

The Purser smiled.

"One is an Egyptian gentleman who will be leaving us at Alexandria, and the other . . ."

He looked down at his desk as if searching for the name, and the Duke held his breath.

It seemed as if an eternity passed before the Purser found the piece of paper he wanted and said:

"The other is a Miss Vina Wallace, who is travelling alone."

The Duke, holding the Passenger List, gave no indication of his relief.

He knew, however, that his intuition had been right and that he had found Vina.

Only when he was settled into his comfortable quarters and Hodgson, having supervised the arrangements in his Sitting Room, was unpacking in his bedroom, did he ask himself how soon he should approach her.

It would be a mistake to do so at once.

When he thought of it he was half afraid because, if she was upset or frightened by his appearance, she might throw herself overboard.

He could remember all too clearly that she had sworn to him that she would not throw herself from the Tower of Despair.

But that would not prevent her from throwing herself into the sea, or taking her life by some other means.

"I have to do this very carefully and cleverly," the Duke mused.

He thought that when he talked to her he might persuade her to leave the ship at Gibraltar, and that they could return to England either by sea or by land.

He therefore had dinner in his Stateroom and retired to bed, wondering what was happening at Quarington and how John Simpson had coped with the General and Lady Wallace.

Whatever his intentions had been for the next day, they were frustrated by a storm that blew up overnight.

The *Magnificent* rolled and pitched as it passed down the English Channel and, by the time they reached the Bay of Biscay, it was difficult for anyone to move about.

The Duke was a good sailor, but he was not so foolish as to risk breaking a limb by doing so unnecessarily.

He therefore stayed comfortably in his cabin, merely instructing Hodgson to find out from the stewards what he could about Vina.

Hodgson was a past master at espionage, and came back with the information that Vina was in a cabin not far from the Duke's.

"The Stewardess tells me," he said with a grin, "that Miss Vina's lying on 'er bed, reading a book, and hasn't got much to say for 'erself."

The Duke thought that that, at least, was sensible.

The next three days, while the storm continued, Hodgson learned that Vina was quite comfortable and had asked for nothing except more books.

"Are there some aboard?" the Duke asked.

It was something with which he had never been concerned on his various voyages.

"There's quite a number, Y'Grace, in the Writing Room, which is at the end of this corridor, although I gather there's not many people interested at the moment!"

Hodgson had already given the Duke a vivid description of how ill most of the passengers were.

It was only when they were not far from Gibraltar that the Duke thought the time had come when he must find Vina and talk to her.

He had eaten a good breakfast and was wondering, now that the sea was calmer, whether he should go out on deck as he was longing to do, when Hodgson came to tell him that Vina had been out very early.

She had now returned to her cabin. The Duke realised he had missed her, and was annoyed.

He walked round the ship several times, feeling better for the air and the exercise, although there was a chill wind.

The majority of the passengers who had struggled up on deck looked "green about the gills," and very chilled from the wind.

The Duke was quite aware that a number of them followed him with their eyes, thinking he was without exception the most handsome man they had ever seen.

He was wearing his gold-buttoned boating-jacket and a peaked yachting cap covered his dark hair.

Yet, now that things were more normal, the Duke was bored.

He wanted to talk to Vina, and he debated for a long time whether to go to her cabin, which would be embarrassing, to or ask her to come to his.

He had the feeling she might refuse, in which case he would have alerted her to his presence aboard quite unnecessarily.

If she hid from him for the rest of the voyage, there was little he would be able to do about it.

As he went below to the Saloon for luncheon, he thought perhaps he would see her in the distance.

It might be easier if he approached her in public, when it was less likely she would make a scene.

He could also prevent her from running away from him.

But there was no sign of her, and he learnt from

Hodgson that she had said she had no wish to leave her cabin and wanted her meals brought to her as they had been during the storm.

The Duke was once again faced with the problem of what he should do.

Then fate played into his hands.

He walked round the deck during the afternoon feeling he needed the exercise and realised even as he did so that the air was growing warmer now that the wind had abated.

The sea was very blue and the sun had emerged far behind the clouds.

He wondered if Vina was aware of it, if she felt that now something had to be done and that he must talk to her.

He left the deck and began to walk along the corridor towards his own cabin.

Then, on an impulse, he walked on to the end of the corridor to where Hodgson had told him the Writing Room was situated.

He had just reached the door, when he heard a woman scream.

Then a man's voice said:

"Come on, now, do not be stupid! You're alone and I'm alone, and if we have a bit of fun together, who's to stop us?"

As the Duke pushed open the door of the Writing Room, which was slightly ajar, he heard Vina reply:

"Go . . . away! Leave me . . . alone!"

He walked in and saw she had been pressed against a wall by a flashily dressed man, who was trying to kiss her.

It took the Duke only two steps to cross the room, catch the man by the back of the collar, and pull him away with a violence which threw him backwards down onto the floor.

He half sat, half lay there with a dazed expression on his face, as if for the moment he did not know what had happened to him.

"Get out!" the Duke said sharply. "And if I see you behaving like this again, I will have you put off the ship at Gibraltar!"

The Duke's appearance, the anger in his eyes, and his voice which was obviously one of authority made the man grunt surlily:

"I did not mean any harm."

"Then get out!" the Duke said again.

Hurriedly the man obeyed, and, as he moved towards the door, the Duke turned to look at Vina.

She was staring at him as if she had seen a ghost, and her eyes seemed to fill her small face.

"It is . . . you!" she said in a voice he could hardly hear.

"Yes, it is I," the Duke replied, "and I obviously arrived at the right moment."

"H-he . . . was trying to . . . kiss me!" Vina whispered, and he saw she was trembling.

"You cannot really blame him," the Duke said gently, "if you are so unwise, looking as you do, to travel alone."

He thought, as he spoke, that she was lovelier than he had remembered.

But once again there was fear in her eyes, and he knew that he wanted to protect her.

Then, as if she could hardly believe he was real, she asked:

"H-how . . . can you be . . . here? How is it . . . possible?"

"I want to tell you all about it," the Duke replied, "and I suggest that if we do not want to be interrupted, we should go to my cabin which Hodgson has transformed into a very comfortable Sitting Room."

"Hodgson . . . is with . . . you?" Vina asked. "And . . . and who . . . else?"

The Duke, reading her thoughts, knew that she was afraid he had brought Edgar with him.

"When I realised where you had gone," he said, "I reached the ship by the skin of my teeth. Only Hodgson is with me."

"Are you . . . saying that you . . . followed me? But . . . how did you know . . . I was . . . here?"

"That is exactly what I want to tell you," the Duke replied, "and I think we would be much more comfortable sitting down than standing here where we may be overheard."

He saw Vina look nervously towards the door, and he knew he had struck the right note.

The ship gave an unexpected lurch, and he put out his hand to take hers.

"Come along," he said, "and although the weather is better than it has been for the last few days, it is still wise not to take risks with our sea-legs."

Vina made a little sound that was almost a chuckle. Then she said:

"I was . . . far too . . . frightened to . . . walk about during . . . the storm."

"So was I," the Duke admitted, "but I was longing to talk to you, and found it very boring to be alone."

He knew without looking at her that she was staring at him in surprise.

Then he drew her out of the Writing Room and along the corridor.

chapter seven

THE Duke opened the door and Vina passed into his Sitting Room.

He shut the door and turned round to see her standing looking at him, her eyes apprehensive and, he thought, still frightened.

He smiled as he moved towards her.

Then, and he was not quite certain how it happened, she was holding on to him and her face was hidden against his shoulder.

He could feel she was trembling, and he said reassuringly:

"It is all right, you are quite safe."

"H-he . . . frightened me," Vina said in a small voice. "He spoke to me on the . . . train and I was . . . afraid if I left . . . my cabin he . . . would be waiting for me."

"You were very foolish to think you could travel alone," the Duke said.

She did not answer; her face was still hidden.

The sunshine coming in through the porthole seemed to envelop her in a golden light.

To his surprise he felt the blood throbbing in his temples and his heart beating frantically.

Then he knew, although it seemed incredible, that he was in love.

It was different from anything he had felt before so far as a woman was concerned.

With Irene Halford and every other woman with whom he had enjoyed passionate *affaires de coeur*, the fire within him had burned fiercely for a short time, then died away, leaving not even a glow in the ashes. Now he knew that he wanted to protect Vina and look after her.

He realised that it was something he had felt for a long time, but had not admitted it to himself.

It was, of course, he now knew, why he had run after her in an impulsive way which was very unlike his usual correct and well-organised actions.

He had also experienced a terror of what might happen to her. He had never felt it for any living person.

The ship rolled a little and he drew her to the sofa.

She sat down, only raising her head as she did so.

He saw there were tears on her cheeks, and he took a fine linen handkerchief from his pocket and put it into her hand.

She wiped her tears away, then she said humbly:

"I . . . I am . . . sorry."

"I wish you had trusted me with what you intended to do," the Duke gently said.

"You would have . . . tried to . . . prevent me," she answered. "I know that . . . you and Aunt Marjory will be

". . . very angry . . . but I cannot marry him . . . I cannot!"

"So you thought you would hide away in India?"

"It is the . . . only place where I . . . know I could be . . . safe and be with people who . . . loved Papa."

"Do you really think it would be possible for you to stay there indefinitely?" the Duke asked.

She did not answer. Then she said almost defiantly:

"I took my . . . jewellery with . . . me."

"The thought of that frightened me more than anything else when I read your letter," the Duke said. "You might have been robbed, and even injured!"

"I had stopped at the Bank," Vina continued, "on my way to London, and I drew a . . . cheque for . . . 500 pounds. I guessed if I . . . asked for more it might seem . . . suspicious."

"I see that you thought out everything very cleverly," the Duke remarked, "but you were not clever enough to realise that you are too young and far too pretty to travel unattached."

Vina made a helpless little gesture as she said:

"I . . . I did not know . . . there were . . . men like the one you . . . saved me from . . . just now."

"Well, now that you do know," the Duke said quietly, "what are you going to do about it?"

He saw the terror once again in her eyes and knew, because he could read her thoughts, that she was thinking that if he sent her back, she must die.

As if she wanted to run away, she rose from the sofa to stand at the window looking onto the deck outside.

It was too high for anyone to look in, but she could see the sea beyond the railing and the white foam of the waves.

"*That* would be a very stupid thing to do," the Duke

said quietly, "and would undoubtedly cause a great scandal."

"I cannot believe ... anybody would worry about ... someone as ... unimportant as ... me," Vina said.

"They would certainly ask a great many questions— why you were with me, and what I had done to upset you."

Vina turned to look at him with wide eyes, and he knew that had not occurred to her before.

When she looked away again, the Duke said:

"I cannot believe you dislike me so much that you would put me in an invidious position for which I would have no reasonable explanation."

"No ... no ... of course ... not!" Vina said quickly. "How could I possibly hurt you when you have been ... so kind to ... me?"

"I am trying to be kind," the Duke said, "but I think we must talk things over and decide what is the most sensible thing to do in the circumstances."

He saw a little tremor go through her. Then she replied passionately:

"I cannot ... go back! I cannot ... marry your ... brother! He is ... horrible, cruel ... wicked!"

Her voice faltered before she continued:

"I heard him say that he would ... spend all the money that ... was Papa's on ... bad women and giving ... riotous parties ... that is wrong ... I know it is wrong!"

"Of course it is wrong," the Duke agreed.

There was a little silence, then Vina said in a hesitating voice, as if she were testing him:

"I want to ... give it to ... children in India ... who are ... hungry."

"I can think of a lot of ways, including that, which your fortune would be of inestimable benefit to those who really need it."

Vina gave a little gasp. Then she turned round to stare up at the Duke.

"Do you . . . mean that . . . do you really . . . mean it?" she asked.

The Duke rose to his feet.

"Of course I mean it," he said, "but it is something that must be done sensibly, and as cleverly as your father managed to help the British authorities when he was alive."

"That . . . is what I . . . want."

She looked up at the Duke, who was standing beside her.

Now he thought her face was changed and there was an expression he had never seen before.

Her eyes met his, and she said in a voice that was a little above a whisper:

"You . . . really will . . . help me . . . you really . . . will?"

"You know I will," the Duke said.

She gave a little cry of sheer happiness.

Then, or perhaps it was because of the roll of the ship, she flung herself against him.

His arms went round her, and as her face was turned up to his, without thinking, because it was what he wanted, his lips came down on hers.

He felt a little tremor go through her.

Then as her mouth, very soft, sweet, and innocent seemed to respond to his, his became more possessive, more demanding.

To Vina it was as if she were swept from the depths

of the darkness of death like depression into the sunlit sky.

*   *   *

She had been terrified at Quarington to the point of killing herself by jumping off the Tower of Despair.

When the Duke had prevented her from doing that, she had suddenly thought that the only way she could save herself was by running away.

She had tried to plan her departure with the same expertise that her father would have used, writing her letters to the Duke and to the Solicitors giving 50,000 pounds to Lord Edgar.

She thought after that they would not be concerned with her anymore.

She had realised that her aunt would be furious, but once she was in India, it might be years before they found her, and a long time before she would have to communicate with them.

It was when she thought of India that it had seemed as if her father were telling her exactly where she would be safe and where no one could force her to marry Lord Edgar.

Her jewellery was so valuable that she knew that if she sold it she could live for a lifetime on the proceeds.

She was sensible enough to realise that she would need money in cash for her fare and her expenses on the voyage.

By questioning her maid, she had learned that there was a train to London, which the servants sometimes caught on their days off, that passed through the Halt at Quarington at dawn.

She also knew where her Bank was situated. It was

fortunately on the way to Fenchurch Street station.

When she caught the train without any difficulty she thought how clever she had been and now everything was "plain sailing."

Although she had arrived from India at Southampton and the S.S. *Magnificent* was sailing the next day, she was aware that she must catch the boat-train to Tilbury.

What she had not anticipated was that travelling alone was very different from journeying with her father, or with the chaperon whom her uncle had engaged to escort her back from India.

As she waited on the platform she had been aware that several men had eyed her in a way that made her feel uncomfortable.

She got into a carriage which was empty except for one lady.

Soon after the train had started, a man, flashily dressed and whom she guessed was a commercial traveller, came in from another compartment and sat down opposite her.

He had insisted on talking to her although she tried to read the newspaper she had bought at the station.

When they arrived at Tilbury he officiously got her a porter and insisted that they walked the short distance to the ship together.

She was able to pay for one of the more expensive cabins, and one was available.

When the steward carried her baggage into it, she thought with relief that she had got rid of the man who had refused to leave her side.

She had hoped he would be travelling in another Class, but unfortunately he was booked into a First

143

Class cabin although she realised that his was not so expensive as hers.

She had, however, no intention of mixing with the other passengers on board and was prepared to stay in her cabin even before the storm sprang up.

Then she had learned from her stewardess that everybody had been advised not to move about.

The stewardess brought her books from the Library and she was happy reading, even though she could not help wondering what had happened at Quarington when the Duke had received her letter.

She wondered, too, if he would be relieved that she was no longer there to cause problems, what he might think of her when he rode *Hercules*.

It was difficult, when the ship pitched and tossed, not to think that she might be riding him over the jumps which the Duke had said were too high and too dangerous for her.

She was sure that it was the most exciting thing she had ever done.

She kept remembering, too, how kind the Duke had been when he had talked to her on top of the Tower, and had prevented her from ending her life as she had meant to do.

On the second day of the storm she received a note from the man who had talked to her in the train and whose name, she learned, was Rawlinson.

Then she had felt a sudden longing for the Duke's protection.

She told herself she was being very foolish to be frightened.

All she had to do was to ignore Mr. Rawlinson's

suggestion that they should meet as soon as she felt well enough.

If she stayed in her cabin, there was nothing he could do to upset her.

She had, therefore, torn up the note and tried to tell herself that she was perfectly safe on her own.

A little later there had been a knock on the door and, when Vina had called, "Come in!" the knock had come again.

It had never struck her for one moment that it might be Rawlinson.

When she opened the door and saw him outside, she gave a little gasp of horror.

"I heard you were not seasick like the rest of the passengers," he said, "so, as we have the ship almost to ourselves, suppose you come and do a bit of exploring with me?"

"No . . . thank you," Vina said firmly.

She would have shut the door but he put his foot inside.

"Come on," he said, "be friendly. I want to talk to you, and I've a great deal to say."

"Will you please go away?" Vina said. "You have no right to come to my . . . cabin . . . as you . . . well know."

"Now you're being unkind," he said accusingly. "There's no one on board as pretty as you are, and if I help you to the Saloon, which is empty, I'll see that you do not fall down."

He put out his hand towards her as he spoke and Vina gave a little cry.

Then, as he came farther into the cabin, she pressed the bell for the stewardess.

As she did so the ship rolled so heavily that she fell

onto the bed; then she realised that Mr. Rawlinson was sitting beside her.

"Go . . . away!" she said angrily. "Go . . . away at . . . once!"

He laughed and put his arms round her. At that moment the stewardess appeared in the open doorway.

Mr. Rawlinson realised he was defeated, and, rising from the bed but holding on to it to steady himself, moved towards the door.

"See you later!" he said. "And perhaps the sea'll be calmer to-morrow. Until then, Toodle-oo!"

He walked out in a swanky manner which was made slightly ridiculous by the fact that only by holding on to the lintel of the door was he able to prevent himself from falling.

The stewardess looked across the cabin at Vina sitting pale and frightened on the bed.

"How did he get in?" she asked.

"He . . . knocked on the door and I . . . thought it was . . . you," Vina explained.

"Well, in future, Miss, I'll bring my key with me, or else I'll tell you who is outside. I know his type, and they're a nuisance on board any ship."

She had gone out and shut the door, leaving Vina alone.

*　　*　　*

When the Duke had saved her from Mr. Rawlinson, she had not been able to believe he was really there.

She knew she was not imagining things—he was alive—but she felt as if he had stepped out of a dream.

It was impossible to look away from him. His eyes

seemed to grow larger and larger until they filled the whole world; there was only him.

As he kissed her, she knew that this was what she had wanted.

Although she had escaped from Quarington and Lord Edgar, she had felt as if something precious had been left behind.

The Duke went on kissing her, and she knew she had loved him for a long time, certainly, although she had not realised it then, since the moment when they had ridden together and she had been afraid because he was angry.

She had never been frightened of him as she was frightened of Lord Edgar.

She could not explain why, when he was in the room, despite her terror of his brother, his presence had given her a feeling of confidence.

It was a feeling of security which somehow resembled what she had felt from her father.

Now she knew it was love.

She felt as if the light from the moon and the stars, which had been so beautiful when they had looked at it together from the top of the Tower, was moving through her body.

"How could you try to leave me?" the Duke asked; his voice was unsteady.

"I love . . . you!" Vina whispered. "I know . . . now that I love . . . you."

"As I love you, my lovely one," the Duke answered.

Then he was kissing her again; kissing her insistently as if he were afraid of losing her, chaining her to him with kisses.

147

Only the roll of the ship made them once again sit down on the sofa.

Now the Duke held Vina close against him and, as her head fell back onto his shoulder, he kissed her forehead, her eyes, her little straight nose, then her mouth.

"How can you be so undeniably beautiful?" he asked.

"I ... I never thought ... you would ... admire me," Vina replied, "when you had ... Lady Halford and all those ... beautiful women to look at."

"Your beauty is very different from theirs," the Duke said, "and you are different from anybody else I have ever known."

Vina drew in her breath.

"Do you ... mean that?"

"I mean it, my darling, and now there are no more problems."

"What ... do you ... mean?"

"I mean," the Duke replied, "that I will look after you, protect you, and keep you from anyone who frightens you."

For a moment he saw a radiance in her eyes that reminded him of the stars; then she looked away, to say in a small voice:

"I was ... going to India ... where no one would ever ... find me."

"Do you really believe I would have allowed you to do that, or that you could manage on your own?" the Duke asked.

She did not answer, and after a moment he said:

"You said you found England dull, but perhaps it will not be so very dull if we are together."

She looked at him a little uncertainly, and he said:

"I am asking you, my precious, to marry me, and that is something I have never asked any other woman!"

"But . . . you cannot . . . m-marry me!" Vina said quietly.

"Why not?"

"Because I am not . . . grand enough . . . and there is . . . Lord Edgar."

"All my brother wants is money," the Duke said in a hard voice. "So, once again, I will pay his debts and he will spend it on women in the irresponsible way which has shocked you."

"I can do . . . that," Vina said.

"As you so rightly thought," the Duke replied, "whatever we give to Edgar is a criminal waste of money, which should be spent on people who really need it."

Vina drew in her breath.

"But he . . . wants money . . . and I think he will be very . . . angry and disagreeable if I . . . married you."

The Duke thought this was, unfortunately, true, but, because he did not want Vina to be upset, he said quickly:

"I am sure we can think of some way of controlling him, but one thing is absolutely certain—you are not going to marry him simply because he is greedy for your fortune!"

Vina gave a deep sigh of relief. Then she said:

"But I am . . . still not . . . important enough to be . . . your wife."

"The only person who can decide that is me," the Duke said firmly, "and I need you, Vina, as I have never needed anyone in my whole life!"

She drew a little closer to him as he continued:

"It was a crazy idea in the first place that Edgar should marry a woman just because she is rich. From the moment I saw you, I knew that for you, it would be impossible."

"Did you . . . really think . . . that?" Vina asked.

"I think I fell in love with you," the Duke answered, "when you came into the Drawing Room looking so beautiful. Then after you had spoken with Edgar I saw the terror in your eyes. I knew then, although I would not admit it to myself, that I had to save you from him."

"You saved my . . . life when we were on the . . . top of the . . . Tower," she murmured.

"I do not want to think of it," the Duke said. "If I had lost you, I would have lost the most precious thing in the whole world!"

He did not wait for her reply, but was kissing her again: kissing her until she felt she was no longer on earth, but flying with him in the sky.

They were enveloped by a Divine Light which could have come only from God.

*   *   *

A long time later the Duke said:

"Do you feel the sea is very much calmer, or perhaps it is because I am happy and all the depressions, doubts, and fears have gone."

Vina laughed and he said:

"Shall we walk round the deck together? To-morrow we arrive at Gibraltar."

He looked at her enquiringly as he spoke, and Vina asked:

"Do you . . . want to go . . . back from . . . there?"

"I was just thinking about it," the Duke said, "and,

as we have the chance of getting to know each other without a great many explanations or interruptions, I suggest, if you agree, my darling, that we go on to Alexandria."

He saw Vina's eyes light up and, before she could answer, he said:

"Perhaps an even better idea would be if we honeymooned in India, and you can show me some of the places where you have stayed with your father. I also have some friends there I would like you to meet."

Vina stared at him in astonishment, then she asked:

"Do you . . . mean . . . that?"

"Of course I mean it!" the Duke said. "And as I can hardly arrive in India alone with a beautiful young woman, even though she is my fiancée, I suggest we are married to-morrow in Gibraltar."

Vina gave a little gasp. Then she said falteringly:

"Is that . . . really possible?"

"I can imagine nothing more wonderful than being married to you," the Duke said, "and I dread the thought of a grand wedding with all our friends speculating as to why we have married each other, and coming to entirely the wrong conclusions!"

Vina laughed, and the Duke said with a note of urgency in his voice:

"What are we waiting for? I love you and I know that you love me. If you can run away, that is what *I* intend to do, and if people complain, we shall not hear them."

Vina gave a little laugh.

Then, as she moved closer to him, she said:

"I, too, would be . . . frightened of a grand . . . wedding and perhaps . . . no one would . . . understand

... least of all Aunt Marjory; but I do ... wish you were ... not a Duke!"

"It is something I cannot help," the Duke said with a wry smile.

"I know," Vina agreed, "but if you were an ordinary man, no one would be surprised at you marrying me ... and they would not ... think I was ... marrying you for your ... title."

"What does it matter what they think?" the Duke asked. "I am not, my lovely one, marrying you for your fortune, or your jewels, and I believe, perhaps conceitedly, that you love me for myself."

"I love you ... because you are the ... most wonderful ... man who ever ... lived," Vina said with a note of passion in her voice, "and my intuition, which you have too ... tells me that we have ... loved each other in other lives ... and I know that this ... life is not ... long enough for me to ... discover how ... marvellous you are!"

The Duke had no words with which to answer this, so he kissed her.

He knew as he did so that this was what he had always wanted.

But he had thought it was impossible to find a woman who loved him completely for himself and actually wished he were not a Duke.

He had been used to women running after him.

Yet he had always been cynically aware that if they were attracted by his looks and because he was an ardent lover, the glamour of Quarington and his social position was indivisible from him as a mere man.

Because, as Vina had said, his perception was acute,

he knew that she loved him in a very different way from that in which any other woman had done.

He had believed her when she said that she would have been content to travel with him about the world as two ordinary people, a man and a woman who had little to recommend them except their intelligence.

Now, because he had been seeking for the end of the rainbow all his life, although he could not actually put it into words, he knew he was inestimably lucky, he went on kissing Vina, aware that she was very young, very unspoilt, and very innocent.

It was what he had always wanted to find in his wife and he knew that at last he had found perfection.

Together he and Vina could spend her money and use his authority to do good in the world, especially in India and in England.

"I love you, my precious!" he said very quietly.

It was not only the truth, but a vow which he intended to keep for the rest of his life.

*   *   *

The ship entered Gibraltar harbour early in the morning and the Rock was looking formidable and golden in the sun.

The sea was blue. Vina looked at the people waiting for the ship to dock, and the Union Jack flying in the breeze. She felt as if everything were enchanted.

Standing on deck beside the Duke, she slipped her hand into his, and, as he looked down at her with a smile, she asked:

"What plans have you made?"

"I will tell you all about them a little later," the Duke said, "and as you will see in a minute, Hodgson will be

153

the first ashore and will carry out my instructions."

"You are making me curious."

"The first thing we have to do," the Duke replied, "is to buy you a wedding ring, and I do not think that will be difficult. At the same time, we have no wish for anyone to be curious about us."

"No . . . of course . . . not," Vina agreed, glancing over her shoulder.

She returned to her cabin and two hours later met the Duke and they went ashore to a jewellers, where he bought her a wedding ring and also a large aquamarine, which she looked at with delight.

"There are a large number of rings at home which have been worn by the family brides," he said, "and I do not presume to rival the jewels which belonged to the Maharajah. But this, darling, is just a small token of my love and my gratitude for the happiness you have already given me."

She looked at him with an expression which made him want to kiss her and, as they left the shop, she asked:

"Where are we going next?"

"The Dean should be waiting for us at the Cathedral, for I have already arranged matters with the Governor," the Duke replied, "and because I think it is a mistake for the people at home to be told what has happened in the newspapers rather than by ourselves, I am being married simply as Alveric Quary."

Vina looked surprised and he continued:

"It is, of course, my name, but without all the trappings, and I think if we are clever, what journalists there are on the island will not suspect for a moment that anything especial has happened."

Vina smiled at him.

"It is much . . . more exciting than a . . . wedding in St. George's, Hanover Square!"

The Duke thought there were few women who would think that when they married him.

He told himself once again that Vina was unique, different from anybody else he had ever known.

The Church, when they reached it, was empty except for Hodgson and the Dean, who was praying at the altar, and somebody playing the organ very softly.

As Vina and the Duke entered, Hodgson presented her with a bouquet of white flowers.

They proceeded up the aisle and the Dean rose from his knees and stood waiting for them.

He was an elderly man, who conducted the Service with a sincerity which made Vina feel that he blessed them with every word he spoke.

When the Duke put the ring he had bought on her finger, she thought it was a fitting symbol that they would be together for ever and nothing would ever part them.

Then, as they knelt for the Blessing, she thought that her father had protected her and brought her the love which he had found with her mother.

She knew she would be grateful for the rest of her life at having found someone who understood her and who she was aware with every instinct in her body was fine and noble.

As they drove back to the ship, she asked:

"What are you going to say to . . . the Purser? Is he to know that we are . . . married?"

"I will tell him after we have left Gibraltar," the Duke said, "and swear him to secrecy. There is no need for anybody else to be aware of what has happened until we reach Calcutta."

"And . . . then?" Vina asked.

"I am afraid, my precious, we will have to stay with the Viceroy for a few nights until we set out to explore the country of which I know so little and you know so much."

"It is so . . . exciting, and I am only . . . frightened I shall not be a good enough . . . guide," Vina said.

"I think that you will guide and inspire me in a great many ways. Seeing India is only one of them," the Duke replied.

They went back to the ship. Then, at last, the Duke was able to put his arms around Vina and kiss her.

"You are my wife," he said, "and I thought I would never find anyone who would be so completely the ideal I have always imagined."

"Oh, darling, I am so afraid of . . . failing you," Vina said, "but I love you with all my heart, and as we were married, I felt Papa was with us, understanding and making sure I would be able to make you happy."

"I never knew what happiness was until now," the Duke said tenderly.

They lunched in their cabin, knowing that the ship was leaving in the afternoon.

The storm in the Bay of Biscay had caused some delay, and the Captain was eager to make up lost time, the next stop being Alexandria.

They were actually out at sea and were sitting talking on the sofa, when a steward came in with a cable.

"I'm sorry, M'Lord," he said to the Duke, "but it's been slightly delayed owing to us 'avin' to leave in such a 'urry."

The Duke accepted the cable with indifference, thinking it would be from John Simpson, wondering if in his reply he should say that he had found Vina.

He had, in fact, not perturbed himself unduly about what might have occurred at Quarington after he had left.

If Edgar was upset, he thought it would do him good, and he was sure that Simpson would have soothed the General and Lady Wallace in his usual tactful manner.

Now Quarington was far away and in their happiness he had no wish to be concerned with anything but his wife.

He therefore put the cable on the table beside him until Vina said a little nervously:

"Perhaps, darling, you should open your cable, just in case it is anything urgent."

"There is nothing more urgent than that I should kiss you," the Duke replied.

As he spoke he moved his lips over the softness of her cheek.

He felt her give a little quiver, and he laughed gently.

"What do I make you feel, my precious?" he asked.

Vina hid her head shyly against his neck as she said:

"Whenever you . . . touch me . . . I feel as if the moonlight is shining within me . . . and then it becomes . . . little tongues of fire."

"That is how I want you to feel."

He would have kissed her again, but Vina moved from his arms.

"I must go to change for dinner," she said. "I know we are dining in here . . . but I want to look very beautiful for you. After all . . . it is our . . . wedding night!"

157

"A wedding night we will always remember," the Duke said gently.

He thought the smile she gave him as she moved across the cabin was so lovely that he wanted to spring to his feet and pull her back into his arms.

Then, as she disappeared, he rang the bell for Hodgson.

He ordered delicacies for dinner which would not be on the menu, and also tried to think of other ways by which he could please Vina on the first evening of their married life.

"I love her! God, how I love her!" he said to himself.

Then, as he returned to the sofa, he saw the cable where he had flung it down on a side-table. Casually, he opened it.

He looked first at the end. As he had expected, it came from John Simpson. Then he read:

Deeply regret to inform you that Lord Edgar was thrown while riding Hercules late yesterday evening. His Lordship broke his neck, but the stallion is unharmed. Arranging for the funeral to take place on Saturday. Will explain your absence due to being abroad.

John Simpson

The Duke stared blankly at the message.

He was sure that Edgar had deliberately ridden Hercules to defy him.

He had given orders that no one should ride the stallion but himself because the animal was dangerous.

158

Edgar was not a good rider and took absurd risks when he was drunk.

Walking across the room, he shut the cable away into a drawer of the writing-table.

He had no wish to tell Vina, tonight of all nights, of what he had just learned.

At the same time, whilst it made everything easier for the future, it would be a great mistake for their marriage to be announced for some months.

As he thought of it, he realised with a faint smile that it was exactly what Vina would prefer.

Instead of being greeted in Calcutta as the Duke and Duchess of Quarington, as he had intended, they would remain anonymous.

They would explore India and be like two ordinary, unimportant people who would be left undisturbed.

The Duke felt that Fate, perhaps God, had given him a wedding present more appropriate than any other.

It would have been hypocritical to say that he regretted the death of his brother.

Edgar had never been anything but a trouble and a spendthrift ever since he had grown up.

He had been an unhappy, disreputable creature whom no one would mourn except perhaps the Cyprians who had made him spend so much money.

He felt, too, that Quarington would be a happier place without him, while the gossips, who continually gloated over his outrageous behaviour, would find somebody else to talk about.

The Duke said a prayer of thankfulness that it was all over. Now there would be no more scandal, no more strain on the family resources.

"I have been incredibly lucky," he told himself, "I can never be sufficiently grateful."

*   *   *

After a candlelit dinner together in the cabin, filled with flowers which Hodgson had bought at Gibraltar on the Duke's instructions, Vina looked at her husband with a happiness that seemed to vibrate from her like starlight.

"Are you happy, my darling?" the Duke asked.

"So happy that I am afraid I shall . . . wake up and find it had . . . all been a . . . dream."

"You will not do that," he answered, "and now I think that as we have had a long day with a lot of excitement, we should go to bed."

He loved the colour that rose in her cheeks and the way she suddenly looked shy.

By the grace of good fortune, the passenger in the cabin next door to those occupied by the Duke had left the ship at Gibraltar.

This meant that he had a dressing room while Vina had the one next door.

She had changed for dinner, as he had asked her to do, in her own cabin.

When she went into the Duke's, she understood why he had wanted her not to see it beforehand.

While there had been very beautiful flowers around them when they dined, his cabin was decorated with white lilies and white roses.

She looked at them with delight.

Then she realised that the bed was covered in one of the exquisitely embroidered Chinese shawls that had been on sale in the shops as they passed down Main Street in Gibraltar.

She had admired them but had not liked to say so in case the Duke felt she was asking for one as a present.

Now one was spread over her bed and she thought it transformed the cabin into something very lovely.

"How could you make it so beautiful?" she asked.

The Duke, who had followed her, put his arm around her and said:

"I tried to think of a bower for the most beautiful woman I have ever seen!"

She gave a little laugh. Then she said in a low voice:

"And the most . . . wonderful man . . . alive."

* * *

Very much later, when the ship was moving in smooth water so that there was hardly any movement, Vina stirred in her husband's arms.

"I want to say I love . . . you," she whispered, "but you have . . . heard it before."

"I can never hear it too often," the Duke answered, "and I love you, my precious, and will love you until the stars fall from the sky and the seas run dry!"

"That is what I want you to say . . . but I was so . . . afraid I might . . . disappoint you."

"How could you possibly do that?"

"I know how ignorant I was about love," Vina said, "but I had no idea it was so exciting and . . . so wonderful! At the same time . . . because you are so experienced . . . you might have found me . . . boring."

The Duke laughed, and it was a very tender sound.

"That is one thing you will never be, my precious," he said, "not only as regards love, but also in everything you do, everything you say. You have always been original, unusual, and different, and that is how I want you to be."

"Could anything be more different or exciting than our being married as we were . . . and having . . . a honeymoon where no one can . . . interrupt us?"

"No one shall ever do that," the Duke said, "and I agree with you that we are starting off on an adventure not only on our honeymoon, but also in our future life."

He felt her move a little closer to him and he said:

"I have not forgotten that you found England dull."

"That was because I had not found you," Vina said simply. "I know now that whether we were living on the top of a mountain or at the bottom of the sea, anywhere would be exciting if you were there."

The Duke kissed her forehead as he said:

"I hope you will always go on thinking that because you are so lovely that I shall always be afraid of losing you."

He was teasing her, but Vina said:

"How could I think or imagine that any man could be as wonderful as you . . . I am the one who is frightened."

"Of what?"

"Other women! Of course they will want you . . . and I shall be . . . terrified that you will prefer . . . them to me!"

"That is impossible," the Duke insisted.

"Why?"

"Because, as you know, if you think about it, we are now not two people, but one. You belong to me, Vina, not only because you are my wife, but because our intuitions are the same, and our hearts and our souls complement each other."

Vina gave a little cry of happiness before she said:

"That is what I want you to think. That is what I believe, but I was so afraid you would not understand."

"Of course I understand," the Duke said. "I understand, too, as the Indians would, that we have been travelling towards each other for centuries, perhaps longer, and, since now at last we have found each other, we can never be parted or separated again."

He knew as he finished speaking that Vina looked up at him, waiting for his lips.

Then, very slowly, as if he wanted to savour the moment, and was thinking over what he had said, he kissed not her lips, but the softness of her neck.

Then, as he felt her quiver he kissed the hollow between her breasts.

Her breath came quickly and he knew her heart was beating as frantically as his.

His hand was touching her, his lips were wooing her, and the starlight moved within them both and became little tongues of flame.

As the Duke made Vina his, they were swept up into the sky, where they touched the stars, held the moon in their arms, and the love of God was theirs for all eternity.

ABOUT THE AUTHOR

Barbara Cartland, the world's most famous romantic novelist, who is also an historian, playwright, lecturer, political speaker and television personality, has now written over 500 books and sold over 450 million books the world over.

She has also had many historical works published and has written four autobiographies as well as the biographies of her mother and that of her brother, Ronald Cartland, who was the first Member of Parliament to be killed in the last war. This book has a preface by Sir Winston Churchill and has just been republished with an introduction by Sir Arthur Bryant.

Love at the Helm, a novel written with the help and inspiration of the late Admiral of the Fleet, the Earl Mountbatten of Burma, is being sold for the Mountbatten Memorial Trust.

Miss Cartland in 1978 sang an Album of Love Songs with the Royal Philharmonic Orchestra.

In 1976 by writing twenty-one books, she broke the world record and has continued for the following nine years with twenty-four, twenty, twenty-three, twenty-four, twenty-four, twenty-five, twenty-three, twenty-six, and twenty-two. She is in the *Guinness Book of Records* as the best-selling author in the world.

She is unique in that she was one and two in the Dalton List of Best Sellers, and one week had four books in the top twenty.

In private life Barbara Cartland, who is a Dame of the Order of St. John of Jerusalem, Chairman of the St. John Council in Hertfordshire and Deputy President of the St. John Ambulance Brigade, has also fought for better conditions and salaries for Midwives and Nurses.

Barbara Cartland is deeply interested in Vitamin Therapy and is President of the British National Association for Health. Her book *The Magic of Honey* has sold throughout the world and is translated into many languages. Her designs "Decorating with Love" are being sold all over the U.S.A., and the National Home Fashions League named her in 1981, "Woman of Achievement."

In 1984 she received at Kennedy Airport America's Bishop Wright Air Industry Award for her contribution to the development of aviation; in 1931 she and two R.A.F. Officers thought of, and carried, the first aeroplane-towed glider air-mail.

Barbara Cartland's Romances (a book of cartoons) has been published in Great Britain and the U.S.A., as well as a cookery book, *The Romance of Food*, and *Getting Older, Growing Younger*. She has recently written a children's pop-up picture book, entitled *Princess to the Rescue*.

In January 1988 she received "La Médaille de Vermeil de la ville de Paris." This is the highest award to be given in France by the City of Paris.